AMIAS:
A WIDOW'S OIL NOVELLA

Ricardo LaVaughn

LaVauri
PUBLISHING HOUSE
LaVauri Publishing House

Amias: A Widow's Oil Novella
Paperback Copyright 2024
©Ricky LaVaughn ©LaVauri Publishing House

All rights reserved. No part of this book may be reproduced, stored in a retrieval system, or transmitted in any form or by any means without the prior written permission of the publisher except by a reviewer who may quote brief passages in a review to be printed in a newspaper, online, blog, magazine, or journal.

Printed in the United States of America

Published by LaVauri Publishing House
www.lavauri.com

Characters are inspired by events told in the Bible.
Scriptural texts are listed below.
The majority of the characters are fictional and the author's imagination.

Cover Designed by Ricky R. LaVaughn
Artwork Photos: Tzvi Eliav

Amias is inspired by 2 Kings 2

"Amias" website:
https://lavauri.com/amias.html

The Widow's Oil series of books:
https://lavauri.com/thewidowoil.html

THE WIDOW'S OIL SERIES

The Widow's Oil series consists of multiple books based on characters and places from the primary novel. Below are a list of some of the books.

PRIMARY NOVEL:
The Widow's Oil

NOVELLAS:
Amias
Rashida
Phashar
Sandstorm

SHORT STORY:
Mary's Tales: Greatness and Treachery

ACKNOWLEDGEMENT

I must thank Jesus Christ for the inspiration and ability to write this novel. It's been a long journey but a fun one. Also, thank you so much to everyone who has encouraged me through your words, text messages, and social media. It means a lot to hear someone say kind words or something positive. Writing a book can be arduous and mundane. However, seeing optimistic messages can give a person that extra oomph to write one more word, page, and chapter, eventually becoming one more book. Thank you again for your support, and continue to be excellent.

DEDICATION

I'm dedicating this book to all those who proceed to do what is right despite danger. It's tough to stand for morals or be a positive influence. Never give up, and keep on being the person this society needs.

TABLE OF CONTENTS

Chapter 1	7
Chapter 2	24
Chapter 3	32
Chapter 4	38
Chapter 5	42
Chapter 6	49
Chapter 7	58
Chapter 8	65
Chapter 9	72
Chapter 10	79
Chapter 11	84
Chapter 12	93
Chapter 13	100

CHAPTER 1

"You one of them prophets visiting our town?" a fruit merchant asked.

"Yes," Amias answered. "Jericho is a beautiful place." The fruit merchant nodded and made an odd sound of agreement. Amias looked over his dull grey and brown robes, which had the tinge of anointing oil in the threads. He touched his greying beard, which needed to be cleaned after a journey from Hazor, a city several days to the north near the Sea of Galilee. Amias had his travel bag with him but didn't think that would have signaled him as a traveling prophet.

Amias spent most of his time in Hazor, a bustling city with various farms, merchants, and metal workers. He was from a smaller city on the sea called Rakkath. He spent his younger years there but felt the call from God to visit and spread His love to as many as possible. Israel, his homeland, was a tapestry of various beliefs, with followers of Baal, Chemosh, Molech, and multiple deities from Egypt. Amias knew that as the country was influenced by the leaders of the land, the prosperity and peace would sway with them. He knew that prophets such as himself and many others throughout the land had to be the lamp bearer for the one true God and the anointed people dedicated to Him.

Although he lived in Hazor, Amias would travel to Dan, one of the northern cities in Israel,

THE WIDOW'S OIL

and Kedesh. However, He visited the coastal towns and cities near Philistia and even went to the towns in Judah, their brethren who had their own kings and queens after the split following King Solomon's reign. Jericho was no mystery to him as one of his best friends, Afra, lived in the large town and was a prophet himself. He didn't think his friend would have announced his coming, so he wasn't sure what the merchant was referring to.

"You don't fit the usual prophet mold," the merchant observed. "A lot of prophets have been passing through these past few days. I took a guess." He wrapped Amias' order of three apples, two peaches, and a kiwi in a silk cloth, a departure from his usual routine. Amias, who was getting the fruit for his friend who lived in town, was intrigued by the sudden surge of prophets in Jericho.

"Is there any particular reason why?" Amias asked.

"Huh," the merchant replied. "Reason for what?"

Amias sighed and glanced around the central area of Jericho. It was full of various stands selling fruits, jewelry, weapons, animals, clothes, oils, and possible little items that he hoped were art pieces but most likely were mini-gods. Each stand had colorful banners with bold lettering to lure people into buying their goods. Of course, everyone said they had the best items, tastiest food, or shiniest adornments.

Getting into the city was not a problem for him. He knew there would be guards posted at both sets of gates. Two walls surrounded the city. The outer wall was older but still useful for defense against attacks. It was near the Jordan River, which provided fresh water, food, and a modicum of protection. The inner walls were perfect for those with more money. They had homes with courtyards for cooking to alleviate smoke in the house, and a few even had two levels to their dwelling to show off wealth and keep their homes cool when it got hot. More importantly, it kept many of the poor and unwanted away from their large domiciles.

Both gates had guards to ensure no one would cause rioting or problems. A few years ago, some people from Moab tried to kidnap an official's daughter for money while she was preparing for her wedding. The guards quickly got the men, and to Amias' knowledge, they were never heard from again. He wasn't sure if they were sent back to their homeland or dealt with according to what the official believed was right. Regardless, more guards were placed around the large gates to protect troublemakers from the city.

"You said a plethora of prophets is visiting Jericho," Amias started. "Is there a new festival or celebration that will take place?"

"Don't think so," the merchant replied. "At least not involving you or people like you."

The comment took aback Amias. Jericho was in Israel. This was his homeland. Every Israelite could trace their lineage to a specific tribe or son of Israel. They were all united as one people, but there was pride amongst each group, where they were from, and what that meant to their family. Amias was from the Naphtali tribe in Rakkath, but even the cities of Hazor and Kedesh were in this group's domain. Jericho sat near the middle of the tribe of Benjamin's territory. He might not have been from Jericho or the tribe of Benjamin, but he was most certainly an Israelite.

"People like me?" Amias asked.

"Yeah," the merchant responded. He looked over Amias' shoulder to another customer who was inspecting the kiwi. His eyes squinted and opened once the new customer nodded that they were interested. "One of them Yahweh believers instead of Baal or Chemosh or whatever."

"Oh," Amias replied with understanding. He tugged on his robes, thought about his greying beard, and nodded. His robes and clothes were made for comfort and reflected his relationship with God. However, the Baal priests had more flash in their outfits, adorned with gold and jewels on their bodies and tattoos covering their skin to honor their god. Amias showing up in his toned-down outfit meant he immediately revealed to whom he worshiped without opening his mouth.

"If you need more of that sweet fruit, come to me, Cowdiy," the merchant said.

"Thank you, and I will," Amias responded while raising the bag.

Amias made his way through the exceptionally large city of Jericho. Many towns throughout Israel and Judah had hundreds of people living there, many only numbering a thousand. However, there were more than four to five times that number of residents. With guests, travelers, and families from other cities coming, the population expanded to almost twice the average. Jericho was one of the first settlements for the Israelites and became an essential place for trade and commerce.

The rebuilt walls were spectacular, and people from all over the nation and surrounding areas called the city their home. Amias was thrilled that he didn't have to enter the second set of gates on this trip, but Afra had taken him into that area years ago to visit a rich friend whose brother, Upaz, lived in Rakkath. Both were quite wealthy, and Amias remembered how Upaz did his best to become one of the region's premier merchants and trading partners. When Amias entered the city, he had to walk to the opposite side of town to get to Afra's dwelling.

Amias could smell a large lamb being roasted over an open flame near a seller providing cooked meats to travelers, visitors, and citizens. It looked fresh as many hunters lived in Jericho to offer wild animals to the city's merchants, eateries, and inns. The cooked lamb was near one of the largest inns in the town, and guards were stationed in front of the building. Carved images lined the pathway while flowing drapes colored in reds, blues, and greens hung on the outside. It was very appealing, and Amias desired to try their food. But he was running late and wanted to get to his friend's home before evening.

After traversing through the city, Amias got to Afra's home near a group of five houses, all close with minimal land around them. The homes were built by a family who lived close to one another, but eventually, various merchants bought the buildings for themselves. They didn't need the land for growing fruits or livestock to graze. Except for Afra, all of them were into trading goods between cities, tribes, or nations. Only Amias' friend was unique with his job compared to their neighbors.

THE WIDOW'S OIL

Amias saw Afra in the front of the home, removing random pieces of what he assumed were trash. They met by chance decades ago when both worshipped in Jerusalem for the Day of Atonement. Jerusalem was in Judah, God's ordained place of worship, which King Solomon built. After the tribes of Judah split with the remaining Israelites, the new king of the northern group, Jeroboam, created two new centers for worship in Bethel and Dan. He was nervous about people traveling from the newly created nation to Jerusalem and overthrowing his power. The latest places of worship were dedicated to false gods, so prophets such as Amias and Afra, along with thousands of others, still made their way to Jerusalem. They talked and bonded over their love of God and the Kiwi fruit. Afra looked up and stopped what he was doing to greet Amias. This made him smile, as he hadn't seen his friend in years.

"It's good to see you Afra," Amias said. The two men greeted each other and began to walk into the home.

"Is this for us?" Afra asked with a pleasant tone.

Amias smiled and handed the man the silk bag of fruit. "Of course, I wouldn't imagine coming empty-handed."

"You're too kind," Afra responded, leading the way inside his house. It was small, with enough room for Afra and his wife Bara. They had no children, so they never needed a reason to add to the home as was customary. Amias was in the same situation as his friend. Although both were in their fifties, they did not have children or heirs. It was not due to them choosing to go without children; it was more like the situation never happened.

Afra was at least married while Amias was still the traveling bachelor, spreading the love of God to all he met. In his twenties, he was betrothed to a woman from Kedesh. Before they were married, a terrible accident happened on her family's farm, and she died from the incident. Amias was encouraged by his family and friends to find another, but he dedicated his mission to God and knew that when it was time, the Lord would provide. It was soon after that he did have to move. His life in Rakkath was great, but emotions were there despite her never living in the home. He didn't want to go to Kedesh, although her family was willing to take him in. So, he decided on Hazor, close enough to both cities but still far enough away to have a clear mind and peace.

"Bara, you remember Amias," Afra said. Bara was a few years younger than Afra, but they both had the same gleam in their eyes and grey hair. Her hair was longer, and her clothes were the color of dew-covered fields, but the texture was thick and partially rough. Afra handed Bara the silk package, and she took it with the same smile and pleasant expression as her husband.

"It's been some years," Bara said and greeted Amias. Her youthful appearance was revealed as she warmly showed kindness. "Please sit, and I'll bring over some refreshments," Bara said.

"Thank you," Amias said.

"Kiwi." Bara held the fruit in the air for Afra to see.

"My favorite," Afra said. "You're the best, thank you."

Amias nodded at the compliment and relaxed in the chair. As Amias remembered the last time, the place was mildly decorated, with various family heirlooms and gifts from people in Jericho. The central room had a table, chairs, and a relaxing couch where guests could rest. To the back were rooms for Afra and Bara to sleep, while the other was where he conducted business, or family could stay there for an extended period. There was a place to cook food and boil tea for refreshment. The courtyard in the back could also be used for more elaborate meals, such as the lamb he saw entering the city.

Like Amias, Afra was a prophet. However, he hadn't traveled as much since being married to Bara. He preferred attending to the people in Jericho and the people in Judah and Israel who lived on the border of both regions.

Bara served Amias a refreshing water with freshly squeezed lemon and lime. It had been a while since he had the lime and enjoyed the delicious drink. He had been actively traveling with people in caravans, on carts, donkeys, and by foot, so sitting and resting felt amazing to his legs and lower back. The refreshing water Bara served helped settle his insides and made him think of what Cowdiy said.

"Is there a celebration or reason for a large gathering of prophets coming to Jericho?" Amias asked.

Afra quickly sucked his teeth and looked at his wife. He returned his gaze to Amias and nodded. "I almost forgot," Afra said.

"There is?"

"No," Afra responded. "But there are a lot of prophets."

Amias scratched his head, puzzled by the response. There seems to be a reason, Amias thought, for a group of prophets in the region to all converge into one city. If it were Jerusalem, it would have made sense to worship or celebrate a particular Sabbath. At least if they were in Bethel or Dan, there would have been some for doing the same with a different set of beliefs. Amias racked his mind and couldn't figure out what would have drawn enough people that a fruit vendor would have noticed. "Am I missing something?" Amias asked.

Afra drank from his citrus-infused water and sighed. "There's a council; we're meeting at the White Owl Inn."

Amias tapped his head and then scratched his beard. He didn't remember the White Owl Inn the last time he visited the city. There were at least three, if not four, spread throughout Jericho. Many large settlements had inns for guests and visitors. Often, people would travel to a city and stay with family, but there might be places where a person, merchant, or traveler doesn't know anybody. The smaller cities and villages might have one inn or none at all. Such an expense didn't make sense if no one was regularly coming.

"The White Owl Inn?" Amias asked. "Is it new?"

THE WIDOW'S OIL

"Yes, maybe a year old," Afra responded. "A consortium of merchants from Manasseh, Gad, Reuben, and possibly people from Ammon all came together to buy the old inn and make it more pleasing."

The first three groups were all tribes within Israel. Everyone was in the northern kingdom of Israel, but their territory rested on the East side of the Jordan River. Most of Israel and Judah were on the west side of Jordan. Ammon was another country whose ties to Israel were complicated due to the various issues, wars, and problems between the two nations.

"What was it before?" Amias asked.

Afra paused for a moment, sipped on his water, and said, "It was an inn. But there was a lot of carousing and partying." Afra drank the rest of his water and let out a huge sigh. "It's not far from here. I remember when some of the worst offenders would cause problems in the street." Bara made a noise, signifying that she had agreed. Amias took a sip and nodded.

"So, it's better now?"

"Much better. They cleaned it up, removed the former staff, changed the look, and now made the place more inviting to guests and residents."

"That's good," Amias said.

"Yes, and we have a council to meet. One of the owners gave us a large meeting room," Afra said.

"Me as well?" Amias asked.

"Yes," Afra started, "you're a prophet."

Amias drank the rest of his water and sighed. The drink was genuinely refreshing, and he enjoyed every single drop. "What's the meeting about?"

"Many believe Elijah will be taken away tomorrow."

****

Elijah was one of the preeminent prophets of Yahweh. Many of the prophets knew of his boldness in talking with royalty and his ability to show the spectacular side of God. He was known for miracles, but one of his most outstanding achievements was his spiritual battle with the prophets of Baal. Like many of the prophets in Israel, Elijah was tired of the continuous worship of Baal. This was due to various kings but was pushed the most by Queen Jezebel from Phoenicia.

The man of God, Elijah, fearlessly challenged the Baal prophets to a spiritual duel to see whose God would accept a sacrifice with fire. Despite their earnest efforts, the Baal prophets did not receive a flicker of flame, while a rush of fire, a testament to the power of Yahweh, consumed the animal, wood, and stone. After this awe-inspiring display, hundreds of Baal prophets met their end. This act of courage and faith caused Queen Jezebel to be furious and hunt him and any other believer down for execution. It was a moment that stirred the hearts of many, causing some Baal believers to turn to Yahweh.

Having escaped the queen's onslaught, Elijah hid in the land for years. Amias, who wasn't sure when Elijah got an apprentice named Elisha, was called while working in his father's fields and followed the prophet. They went on trips to spread the message of the Lord. Afra explained that many prophets in the area had a feeling from the Lord that an event would happen with Elijah. This anticipation of future events caused many from Jericho and the surrounding areas to congregate and talk with the man himself or Elisha about what they believed would happen. The air was filled with intrigue and anticipation, a feeling that Amias found both exciting and unsettling.

"Men, I want to introduce my friend from the north, Amias. We've traveled much of this land informing everyone we meet about God," Afra announced to the council. The room was filled with general greetings, creating a warm and welcoming atmosphere in the enormous space of the White Owl Inn. Amias, a seasoned traveler, was used to the various Inns and communal places around the country. The White Owl Inn, with its basic room for eating, entertainment, and resting, was no different. However, what set it apart was the sense of unity and community among the believers, a feeling that Amias found comforting.

While the earlier inn Amias saw draped their building with bright, bold colors, the White Owl Inn was painted and covered in silver and white. Amias assumed the drapes were changed often to avoid looking stained or dirty. Outside the inn was a giant statue made to look like the White Owl, with its flattened face, large eyes, and sharp beak. Amias had only seen the animal once and thought it had a peculiar look compared to other owls, ravens, quails, pigeons, and falcons. He asked Afra if the man-size statue was worshipped, and he answered that it was only used for decoration and not to be praised.

The room where the council took place was large and moderate in design. It was made for groups and families around the area to meet. However, a place that could have comfortably accommodated thirty to maybe forty people was now housing at least fifty or more. The generated body heat made it challenging for Amias, who was dabbing his brow, to stop the sweat from entering his eyes.

Before Afra introduced Amias to the prophets, he gave some insight into the major power players in the group. Afra explained that most prophets in the room hailed from Jericho, Jerusalem, and Shiloh. However, some heard the news of Elijah as far north as Hazor, which surprised Amias because he was unaware, and Dan, who was even further away. There was a large contingent from Bethel and the cities boarding the Philistine's border.

"It's been brought to my attention that many of you want to harass Elijah's understudy regarding the Lord taking the prophet away tomorrow," Khahea said. His voice boomed through the room, silencing the crowd. Khahea was a sizeable man with dark blue robes and an orange sash. He was the prophet for wealthy merchants and medical professionals near Jericho. They wanted to ensure their communication with God was strong and that their prophet reflected their wealth, status, and relationship with Yahweh.

"It's not harassing," Meonothai said. He was a young prophet whose beard had no speck of grey streaming through it. He was small but appeared to have great strength, as he used to cut parts of the forest down for homes in Jericho and Shiloh. "We're inquiring of Elisha regarding his master."

Khahea snorted at that comment and shook his head. "We shouldn't bother Elisha or set our life to the belief of Elijah being taken away."

"All of these people came for a reason," Afra mentioned.

"We need to get on one accord and then go back into the nation spreading God's word," Khahea snapped.

Amias was confused about why Khahea quickly prevented anyone from inquiring about Elijah. Of course, the prophets would be concerned. Why is he being taken away? Where is the Lord taking him? What is going on? All of these questions cycled through Amias' head but he finally settled on one. "Why is this a problem?" Amias asked.

Multiple people tried to answer and gave a variety of answers. Amias could hear some say that if God impressed upon so many of a miraculous event tomorrow, they should go; others were curious to see where God would take him, and another group wanted to ensure the feeling they had was not false.

"Confusion," Khahea said. "This is why we need to have a mindset that if God decides to take Elijah, we need to move on and do what we can for the Lord. Certainly, he will raise another in his place." Khahea sat up and smiled.

"I think you're just scared," Afra whispered. Amias' head snapped in Afra's direction. He was shocked at the brazen idea of calling someone scared in front of a group of peers. Afra must have thought the ambient noises would cover his comment, but he relayed that message at absolute silence.

"Excuse me," Khahea gritted.

Amias looked at Afra, who opened his mouth and shut it again. He was glancing around the room, afraid to say what he felt. Amias knew some of the men, but most were from a different region than his own. To Afra, his comment or how he came across one of the prophets could label him in a bad light. They might not want to work with him or deal with his ministry. Amias, however, was from a different part of the land.

"He said you were scared for reasons unknown to me," Amias boldly announced.

Khahea's eye twitched at Amias' statement. The temperature in the room seemed to increase by a few more degrees, causing Amias to dap his brow even more. He wanted to be bold and courageous, not accidentally show fear by blinking in pain due to sweat entering his eyes.

"You're not from around here," Khahea said. "What do you know about these surroundings?"

"Enlighten me. What is there to fear?" Amias asked.

"There are some enemies of Elijah who weren't too pleased with what he did to the Baal priests," Meonothai answered.

"You're worried about some Baal sympathizers?" Amias asked.

"Like I said, you're not from here," Khahea said. "Maybe there's no problem in Hazor."

"There's problems everywhere," Amias mumbled.

"Not like here," Khahea shouted. "There is danger everywhere. It will do us no good to end up on the wrong side of the ground, causing confusion and anger amongst those we live around. It would be bad for our lives and the people we represent."

Amias thought about the last part of the phrase. The people we represent. Khahea represented those with money and had much to lose if Baal worshippers or sympathizers decided to either cause harm or stop using their goods. They must have dealt with people who didn't mind them sacrificing to Yahweh as long as they kept in their place. Don't cause a lot of disruption, and everything will be okay. Amias assumed all of this, but knowing what he learned from Afra's background on a few of the people made this clear. He was under no pretense to protect a specific group of people, so there was no fear of reprisals or loss of money.

"I'll see Elisha," Amias said.

Some of the prophets near Amias mumbled at his response with surprise. Khahea and many people agreeing with him sat on the opposite side of the room. They paused in their conversations to look at Amias, the newcomer in town, with disbelief.

"We agreed not to endanger our lives," Khahea said.

"I didn't say you have to go," Amias sneered. "I'm new here, so it doesn't matter. I'll ask

Elisha about God's dealing with Elijah." That response caused more chatter amongst the people about seeing Elisha. Many started to turn from Khahea's point of view. The prophets came from far around; the least they should do was find out for themselves.

"If that happens, then we scour the countryside to see where God will send Elijah," Afra boldly said. Amias hadn't gone that far but nodded in agreement. His friend felt encouraged because there was another who was more than willing to back him.

"You want to go out there," Khahea said, pointing at one of the walls. Amias didn't know which city he was pointing at, and it didn't matter. He and everyone in the room knew that Khahea was referring to the land of Israel far beyond the walls of Jericho. "And begin to announce we're looking for a person they want to kill?"

Amias looked at Afra, who gave a slight nod, and then at Khahea. Before responding, it was the first time he felt a slight comforting breeze brush over his face. He knew it was nothing more than his imagination, but for that moment, it felt great.

"Yes," Amias responded.

Khahea was about to respond when Meonothai agreed to go to Elisha and wanted to visit the countryside. Of course, Afra was about to go since he mentioned it, but many prophets around them also desired to go. People on Khahea's side of the room changed their minds and openly discussed going to Elisha. They did not want to use fear of Baal's followers to stop them. They were prophets

THE WIDOW'S OIL

for Yahweh, which should mean something to the people.

"We can't show fear, Khahea," Amias said. "For our God, ourselves, and the people we represent."

"You don't know what you're dealing with," Khahea responded, pointing at Amias. He was upset that a newcomer had come into his town and convinced people to go in a direction he had not ordained.

"Scared heifers don't produce good milk when it storms," Amias said. "Something my father used to tell me."

CHAPTER 2

"Are you telling us that Elijah is gone?" Amias asked Elisha at his home on a hill near Jericho. The news had struck them like a whirlwind, leaving them in disbelief. He was surrounded by the men from the council the day before. He heard many of them would be there but didn't believe them. Amias assumed he, Afra, and their friend Doro would be the only people showing up. Doro, their best friend, a farmer who lived on the city's outskirts, was also there. He was a tall, muscular man whose rough hands and untamed beard showed the workings of a person who worked in the fields. He stood a full head, taller than most, and his size convinced everyone not to mess with him.

Meonothai, a young man of courage, was among the prophets who visited Elisha. Their actions spoke louder than words, demonstrating their commitment to their faith. They had all gathered to discuss the leadership transition from Elijah to Elisha. Afra, a loyal supporter, was also present and eager to meet Elisha.

Even Khahea was there with the group. His presence surprised Amias. He wasn't sure if it was sincere or to keep his standing amongst the prophets of Jericho and surrounding cities. For most of the prophets, there was a feeling, or some would say a knowledge, that God would take Elijah away. Before Elijah's disappearance, many had talked with Elisha regarding the Lord taking him away.

THE WIDOW'S OIL

When Elijah's final moments became clear, Elisha crossed the Jordan River. Many of the religious and strong men from Jericho and Bethel annoyed Elisha with their relentless barrage of statements and questions. Eventually, only Elijah and Elisha journeyed away from the masses. Amias watched Elisha rub his balding head when he returned, announcing what happened to Elijah. When Amias saw Elisha once before, he thought it was the prophet's choice to be bald. Despite all of Israel's men growing their hair long and healthy, Amias assumed Elisha chose to shave his. Then Amias was informed by Afra that it was not a choice and that Elisha had always had thin or receding hair. There would be a few people in various towns who knew of Elisha's condition and might have some humorous words, but no one would dare say it to his face. Amias always considered anyone who would go against one of God's anointed would have to face the Almighty's wrath.

"God knew that Elijah's time was complete," Elisha answered. More murmurs spread through the crowd. A few men shook their heads, scared of what Elisha meant.

"Complete?" Afra asked. Amias looked at his friend and felt relieved when he said something. He was also about to ask, and Amias could tell many others had their questions. Complete meant that the ministry or mission was finished for that time. However, to Amias and the multiple prophets, priests, and leaders at Elisha's home, it did not appear that the ministry was finished. The people of Israel were still under the pressure of Ahab and

Jezebel. Most of the citizens in Jericho and those in the northern kingdom assumed God would remove the King and replace him with someone who loved the Lord.

"Yes," Elisha started. "Complete. Elijah did what God told him to do. He completed the ministry that God had given and was taken away on a fiery chariot."

The wind felt as though it had stilled with the last part of Elisha's response. Amias looked around, and even the trees paused to avoid swaying. The priest from Rakkath tried to process the idea of someone being taken in a chariot, which was on fire. Was this the same fire used when eviscerating the sacrifice on Mount Carmel? No, that would have destroyed Elijah. Then Amias pondered whether Elisha intended to say that his former master was dead. There was no way Elisha would use a casual tone when speaking of his friend in such a manner. The crowd was silent, each person trying to comprehend the miraculous event Elisha was describing.

"A chariot came and," Amias started, but Elisha raised his hand to stop the question.

"I have his mantel tossed down to me," Elisha responded. The men in the crowd vocalized various amounts of recognition. The mantle symbolized Elijah's authority and power, and its passing to Elisha signified the transfer of leadership. Those in Jericho were more familiar with Elijah's clothes than Amias. He had seen the prophet before but not enough to remember the details of his mantle. To blend, Amias nodded in agreement with everyone else. Afra elbowed him gently, knowing that Amias had no idea if it was the correct mantle or if Elisha was telling a story.

"Are you the new leader?" someone shouted to the left of Amias. Amias turned his head and saw it was Meonothai, the young man from the previous day's meeting. More people muttered to each other about the leadership change and whether Elisha was supposed to take over. Elijah was regarded as a leader amongst those who worshipped Yahweh. Now that he was gone, someone else needed to fulfill that part, which in their minds meant Elisha.

Amias studied Elisha and saw him sigh before preparing his response. He thought about his question when they arrived at Elisha's home and received the news of Elijah. He didn't think about the effects of seeing someone go away without knowing if they would see them again. For most, never seeing a person could mean that they moved to a town in a far-off land or death. For Elisha, it meant seeing your teacher leave in a flaming chariot headed up toward the sky.

"We are all leaders for the one true God," Elisha began. "He has a plan for everyone here. Live to please God so when your ministry is complete, God will look favorably on your life." Amias nodded and thought about the words coming from Elisha. He tried his best to represent God and encourage those who lived near the Sea of Galilee. Many listened and tried their best. Of course, others would go with the influence of the various deities the King and Queen instituted. Amias heard that some people started worshipping gods from other nations boarding Israel. To Amias, enough was enough. He was tired of hearing the stories of his ancestors having a deep relationship with God and the country flourishing while the people in his time did the opposite. A spiritual decay seethed into the people during his time, causing droughts and other nationwide calamities. There were so many people whose morals and values seemed to crumble, and the ideas of countries they were supposed to affect ended up influencing them. Many of the men in the audience nodded in silence at Elisha's statement. And then the silence was broken by a straightforward question.

"How do we know he's not still around?" Doro asked. Amias and Afra looked at their friend and then back at Elisha. Amias agreed. He got caught up in the fiery language and went to the mysticism of something extraordinary happening to the Lord's prophet. Doro, being a farmer, went to the point.

"Because I have told you," Elisha responded. "Why would I lie and communicate a tale of a fiery chariot?" Elisha wiped his brow and said, "Even many of you told me earlier this morning, constantly reminding me that God told you Elijah would be taken away. Often, I said that I already knew and asked you to be quiet. Yet the pestering never stopped."

Elisha was right about that statement. Amias knew there was a feeling amongst the Lord's servants that Elijah would be taken away. God had prepared the prophets for the eventual change of hands, but they could not accurately grasp the significance. The Lord primed them to handle the shift in spiritual presence from Elijah to Elisha; however, once the change happened, the same

THE WIDOW'S OIL

people questioned the validity of what they knew to be true. The leaders were frustrated and wanted clarity.

"Upon going to where Elijah was taken," Elisha started, "we had to cross the River Jordan. Elijah struck it with his mantle; the waters parted, and we walked to the other side. Then, as we traversed, a fiery chariot pulled by fiery horses came from the sky and took Elijah away. He left the one thing I asked for, a portion of his spirit, that power he had resonating within him." The men were hushed during Elisha's speech, clinging to every word as though soothing tones were gracing their ears. "I picked up the mantle and made my way back here, having to strike the River as Elijah had by proclaiming the same God of Elijah is here with me." Elisha paused and wiped his brow again. "Elijah is not here; his mission is finished, and once I crossed and came home, that's when you," Elisha said, pointing to the crowd of men standing around him, "came and asked me of Elijah's whereabouts."

Elisha's story, to most people, would seem fantastical and strange. Parting the turbulent River Jordan with a piece of clothing, being taken away on a chariot of fire, and inheriting a power that gave the wielder abilities more extraordinary than most could imagine. Amias and many religious leaders would not believe it as well if someone other than Elisha had explained their story. However, many of those in the crowd had seen the great acts of Elijah for themselves; they knew there was something special about this prophet, and Elisha's experience with the great man of God was convincing enough.

Amias was familiar with and interacted with Elisha but was not as acquainted as most of the men there. He still believed but had the pull to go and search. He wanted to make sure and see if God had taken Elijah somewhere else. Amias knew that in the distant past, Moses was often led away from the people to receive the laws and commune with God. Having that sort of experience caused a great power to reside in Moses, which altered the course of their ancestors forever. Amias searched for ideas on what to say next. How could he get his point across without sounding ignorant or disrespectful?

"Since there are fifty strong men with your servants," Amias began, "please let us go and search for your master, Elisha."

"Yes," Afra said soon after. Amias was startled by his friend's sudden response but was happy that he did not have to be the only person to have spoken out of turn. "It's possible the Spirit of the Lord has carried him away and put Elijah on the mountains or one of the valleys."

Afra's answer only confirmed what Amias was thinking as well. Elijah could be somewhere else. The fiery, burning, or extremely bright chariot had taken Elijah to another place in the vicinity, and they were supposed to find him. Or at least, he would commune with God and return with an even greater revelation from the Lord. This could be especially true when standing against King Ahaz and Queen Jezebel.

The suggestion rippled from person to person, and a growing excitement cultivated amongst the fifty men. Even Khahea began to come around to the idea and whispered as such to the nearest prophet from Bethel. They thought the idea was great. Looking for Elijah, they could continue their growth in God's power and his never-ending ways to astonish. After only a moment after Afra's statement, Elisha responded.

"Do not send them," Elisha said. Amias felt troubled in his bowels, never thinking that would be the retort. He assumed that Elisha might not be fully on board with the idea but would encourage them to look for Elijah. There was a purpose in finding Elijah, and Amias wanted to be a part of it. However, Elisha's words stunned him and Afra as well.

"It's worth a chance," Khahea said. Others agreed and began pelting Elisha with requests to go. Many of the people mentioned the spiritual strength of finding Elijah. Some talked about the journey being worth returning to God's calling. A group of prophets spoke about wanting to experience Elijah's spiritual power or being in the presence of the Lord's Holy man. While others pseudo did not believe that Elijah was truly gone. After numerous men, including Amias and his two friends Afra and Doro, kept talking to each other and Elisha about the benefits of searching for Elijah, the apprentice finally shouted to get them silent.

"Fine," Elisha bellowed. "Send them."

CHAPTER 3

"Scared cows, produce good milk when it..." Afra started with confusion wrapped across his face.

Amias interrupted, saying, "Scared heifers don't produce good milk when it storms."

Afra roared with laughter, and Bara joined in as well. Their harmonious joy caused Amias to do the same. Bara finished cooking lamb while the two men were sipping tea that contained a little of the kiwi that Amias had bought the day before. Rose petals, a dash of cinnamon, and herbs rounded out the flavor blend. Bara had prepared the beverage the night before when he arrived and had it brewed all day for them after they visited Elisha.

"Did your dad really say that?" Afra asked. The smell of the lamb began to churn Amias' stomach with anticipation. He wasn't hungry when they returned until he smelled the savory meat. Once Bara's cooking took hold of his mind, eating was all he could think about.

"No," Amias responded. "Not to me, and not often. But once he said some combination of that to a neighbor of ours who didn't provide good shelters for their cows."

Afra nodded in agreement and continued to chuckle. "The look on Khahea's face was worth it."

"When was the last time you left Jericho?" Amias asked.

THE WIDOW'S OIL

Afra sucked his teeth and looked up. Amias knew his friend was searching for the answer to that question. Before being married, Afra could travel when he pleased. Then Bara came into his life and didn't move about as much, making Jericho his central area to minister. Amias loved getting on the road to speak about God to whoever would listen and take counsel from the Lord. Nevertheless, there were times when he wanted to be at home and raise some sons. Pass on his knowledge to them in hopes they will grow to be strong young men for God and country.

"A few years," Afra answered. "Not since that swarm came through and tried to inhale our crops. We were in luck that Doro knew the burning branches trick would work."

"Smoke," Amias said. "I have to remember that."

"Hopefully, you will not need it," Afra responded.

"Dinner is ready," Bara said to the men. They prepared themselves and rinsed their hands. They got what they wanted, gave God the praise for the blessing, and of course thanked Bara for her culinary skills. The conversation maneuvered through the various people Amias met on the road. How they are happy to have him in their village or town to give them an encouraging word or blessing from God. Others were steadfast in their belief of Baal, Chemosh, and other gods poured in from the rival nations that surrounded their land. Afra would interject with how he was helping people in Jericho as well as being an inspiration to future prophets to become what God needed them to be. Bara had finished her meal early and went to the spare room in the house, fixing a pair of Afra's shoes for the journey they were about to take.

"Do you believe he's really gone?" Afra asked. The conversation had moved to Elijah and some of the acts they could remember. There were stories of his greatness and some incredible miracles that were performed. Elijah's duel with the Baal prophets did bring some hostile actions toward Yahweh's prophets, but they endured.

"I just want to be sure, or at least see if God has moved him to another part of the land," Amias answered.

"Why?"

"Maybe it's the start of a revival in a new part of Israel," Amias suggested. "God may be using this to get us to battle against an enemy we cannot see."

Afra nodded and sipped on his cooled-off tea. "What if it was time?"

Amias thought about that and nodded. Elisha did have Elijah's mantle and spoke about shifting to a new phase. There was this knowledge that God was moving to a different person to continue what Elijah had done. Still, it was tough to look at it that way. Although Amias knew he didn't have the ability like God to see everything, he had hoped that Elijah's mission would continue. He was older, not all the way old, but there were some vibrant years left to do something amazing for God in Israel. Life is easier when you have a strong trailblazer, charging the way through whatever might influence or affect the leaders and people in the country. Having someone like Elijah meant something, but maybe that was the problem. If people relied on a singular person and not God, then what would that say about them?

"Maybe," Amias said. "Wouldn't you like to know for yourself?"

"Yeah."

"And" Amias started, "all of us men going out into the countryside, to look for Elijah, while also talking and inspiring others about God. How could that be bad?"

Afra nodded at the last statement and drank the rest of his beverage. "I'm glad Doro is coming."

"Same," Amias quickly agreed. Doro with his massive size would be a great deterrent in case the men ran into trouble on the highway to the chosen city. There were robbers and vagabonds lined through the various streets and pathways between towns. Amias always carried a weapon on him in case someone was determined to take what he had. He was very thankful for God's protection, and so far on his journey, he had never experienced trouble. Still, he would rather be safe and have a friend, than be careless and end up broken and robbed.

"He's always working on his farm," Afra said. "Even though he's just outside the city, I rarely see the young man."

Doro was a few decades younger than Amias and Afra. They knew his father and would regularly counsel and bless the leader of the household and his family. Doro took to the scriptures and inspirational talks they would have and even tried teaching his siblings and friends. When Doro became head of the household, Afra remained friends with him as well as Amias. It was easier for Afra since they lived in the same city, but Amias always took it upon himself to be friendly and keep the communication going. Despite the age gap, they shared a deep bond and mutual respect.

"He might be looking for adventure and excitement," Amias responded, and they both laughed.

"Not too much I hope," Bara said entering the main area of the house. She had Afra's shoes in her hand and was heading towards her husband.

"No need to worry Bara, we'll be safe," Afra said. His tone was warm and pleasing. Amias could tell he was reassuring his wife that they wouldn't be in danger.

"How long is this adventurous journey?" Bara asked, placing the shoes in front of Afra's feet.

"Not long," Afra responded and tried on the repaired shoes. "You do such a marvelous job." He pulled Bara close to him and kissed her. "Thank you."

Bara smiled a little and said, "Will you be gone for months?"

"No not at all," Afra responded. He was quick and used more of his assurance tone to slay all fear she might have. Afra hugged his wife and looked to Amias for help. His eyes seemed to pull at his friend to say a few words so Bara wouldn't be scared.

"Yes, exactly," Amias said. "We're going to Naaran, a small village only a day's journey away."

"Naaran," Bara whispered. "Never heard of it."

"I've only known about it in my travels," Amias responded. "After we met with Elisha, Afra, Doro, and I chose Naaran and made it known to the others in the group."

"We didn't want to be too long on the road," Afra reassured.

Bara sighed and kissed her husband once more. "Doro will be with you, so you'll be safe."

"And God," Afra quickly said. "He's always there. We're looking for one of His own."

"Besides, Naaran is a small village that most have never heard of. What danger could we possibly find there," Amias said.

CHAPTER 4

"Doro, the cattle stew was excellent," Amias complimented. "Thank you."

"Don't thank me, thank Lamita," Doro bellowed out. The host, Amias, Afra, and Doro's brother Feidi all laughed. Feidi, who was Doro's younger brother, was a finger shorter than him and had more grey in his beard. Doro's family was large, with him being exceptionally muscular and his brother thicker than him. Lamita, Doro's wife, was built strong and almost the same height as Feidi. She prepared the food with a few of the workers and her sister-in-law.

Doro's home was rounded and sat towards the front of his property. Behind and on all sides was the wheat farm and an area for cattle. Amias remembered when the family started with a few animals. Then, it grew into a major production. The family business expanded, and Feidi and his family lived on the land with several cousins and friends. They provided food for the residents of Jericho, travelers going to Jerusalem for worship, and some who made trips to Bethel.

"Great idea to eat before our journey," Amias said, his voice tinged with anticipation for the adventure ahead.

"I know you wanted to come and go immediately, but I had to give you a little break from your journey thus far," Doro said. His voice was deep, vibrating, and commanding.

Amias was confused, looked in Afra's direction, and then turned his attention back to Doro. "Jericho isn't far from here," Amias said, his voice mingled with curiosity.

"You're only a few stones away," Afra added.

Doro laughed, smacked his leg, and sighed. "Still, who would I be not to entreat friends at my home before we go on our adventure."

"Will you be going far?" Feidi asked. His voice was similar to Doro's. Lamita had reentered the main area where the men sat and ate on the stew.

"Naaran," Amias answered.

"Not far at all," Lamita said. She, like Doro, was quite tall. Lamita rubbed Doro's shoulder as she stood just behind him and smiled. "Before my father arranged our love, we had visited Naaran when I was young."

"She was telling me last night there wasn't much there, but the inn was decent, a deep well for water, some good people, and the food was nice," Doro said.

"As far as I could remember," Lamita responded. "I don't remember it being a major city. Why did you choose Naaran?"

Amias finished the rest of what was in his bowl and said, "We wanted to be close. See if God had sent Elijah somewhere in the region and ensure we return without spending too much time on the road."

"Besides," Doro said and patted Lamita's belly. Amias could barely see that she was with a child when they entered the home. The scent of the food was overwhelmingly good, and he focused his attention on that. Lamita had several more months before God blessed them with a child. "I don't want to miss the birth of another child," Doro finished.

"It's a son," Lamita said.

"I will be pleased with whatever Yahweh provides," Doro said.

"We have three already," Lamita said, referring to the sons Amias remembered seeing throughout the home and land. "We're having a son.

Doro laughed again and smacked his leg in joy. "A mother knows, am I right," Doro told the men. Amias and Afra, not having any children, nodded and laughed in agreement, while Feidi, having multiple sons himself, agreed. To Amias, it was amazing that these two and a few of the cousins he had learned from during their conversation all had sons. He was in disbelief that one family would have all males. Doro even mentioned in their discussion that many people had boys. The farm had plenty of men to work, but they needed women so they could have wives. Getting wives for the men working on the farm was a significant priority for Doro once they returned from Naaran.

"I would love to go with you on this journey," Feidi said, "but my wife is almost ready to bring forth my third."

"God be praised," Afra said.

"Indeed," Feidi responded. "Be safe; a few Baal loyalists might have moved to various villages in this area."

"Feidi, we're not scared of a few bull-head worshippers," Doro said.

Amias thought about how multiple deities in the area all had bulls or calves or bull-head gods. Phoenicia, Moab, Ammon, and even Egypt had gods resembling bulls or cows. The animals were important, but people like Doro saw them as a resource and knew they were nothing to be worshipped or honored. Still, he tried to keep the best cattle for people, using it for food or worship in the temple in Jerusalem or the levities throughout the country. However, he knew some would want his cows and bulls for worship at Bethel and Dan for their sacrifice and belief in Baal and other foreign gods.

"We're looking for Elijah," Amias said. "Not starting any trouble."

"There are some who," Feidi sighed and continued, "are still a little upset at what happened."

"That was years ago," Afra responded.

"Not to the family members of the fallen," Feidi said.

"You're always overly cautious, brother," Doro said. He looked down at his cup and raised it to Lamita. It was empty, and this gesture was his way of asking for it to be refilled.

"Would this give you too much water to carry for such a journey?" Lamita asked.

"There's plenty of trees, I'll be fine," Doro responded. Lamita smiled, shook her head, and left for the area where they kept clean water for a refill. "Besides, brother," Doro continued, patting a large, bladed sword and a homemade blunt weapon beside him. "If there's danger, then may God give me the strength to handle it."

CHAPTER 5

"I think it's going to be a girl," Doro said, breaking the silence. Both prophets were surprised at the sudden conversation change. Amias wasn't sure what Afra was thinking, but they had finished talking about the use of donkeys compared to camels. Doro preferred oxen, but those four-legged animals weren't a part of the original conversation. To Amias, donkeys were helpful due to their hard work carrying various supplies. Mules are even better due to their durability and strength; the inability to make more of them from themselves was a problem. Afra liked Camels due to their ability to go long-range in harsh environments. They could also carry things, including the rider, for extended periods. It wasn't an argument, just a discussion to pass the time.

Amias, of course, realized that they had no animals with them. Naaran was close enough for them to bring supplies, clothes, and weapons. Doro thought about getting one of his carts to take them along, but Naaran, being only a day's journey away, seemed unnecessary. Also, the prophets didn't want to take away any animals or transportation they might need for the farm.

The trio of men had started their journey talking about Doro's sons and the new child on the way, a topic that always brought a sense of anticipation and joy. They briefly mentioned Feidi's concern with Baal worshippers, for which none of them seemed concerned. Then the conversation went to various prophets Afra knew in Jericho, meeting Assyrians in person and even going to a precursor of a battleground. Amias was familiar with that topic due to his experience in pre-war battles when he was only in his twenties. Doro trained to fight but was never part of anything official like war. Amias told them he didn't get a chance to fight in a battle but was besieged once when he traveled with a group of young men on their way to go against the Philistines years prior. Some were making trouble, and he saw firsthand the true horror of war, or at least what death looked like in such a visceral way.

After their discussions on physical and spiritual warfare and the best pack animal, a serene silence enveloped the group. They basked in the tranquility of nature, listening to the melodious chirping of birds and inhaling the sweet fragrance of trees and flowers. The path from Jericho led them through lands filled with the sounds of low grumbles and giant beasts, most of which paid no heed to the travelers. Amias was grateful for the company this time rather than embarking on the journey alone. Doro's unexpected remark about his fourth child was peculiar, but Amias was willing to engage in the conversation.

"What makes you so sure?" Amias asked, his voice tinged with curiosity and a hint of skepticism. "All of yours and Feidi's children are boys."

"Didn't your cousins have sons as well?" Afra asked.

"Yes," Doro responded. "But she will be great. Learn from her brothers and cousins on how to be strong, yet able to be soft like the women on our farm."

Amias nodded and replied, "That would be excellent for her and whomever you marry her to."

"I agree," Doro said and smiled. "She would bring in powerful sons for a good family. To God be the glory."

"Amen indeed," Afra responded.

It was only after a few more paces of taking in the melody of the animals—this time, a few insects were creating songs. Doro broke nature's melody again with a new topic. "You think God would send Elijah in a flaming chariot to Naaran?"

The question had been lingering in Amias' mind as well. He didn't interpret the chariot as being literally on fire. He assumed that Elisha meant it as a metaphor for the intense brightness of what God sent, but with Elijah, anything was possible. Amias was uncertain if Elijah would be in Naaran. God could have placed him anywhere. What part of the city, country, or world, for that matter, was the prophet needed?

"It's as good as anywhere else," Amias answered. "If not here, then any of the multiple groups searching for him will find him."

"And if not," Doro asked.

"Then," Afra started, "it's true. Elisha was right, and Elijah is truly gone."

As they continued their journey, a grasshopper fluttered in front of the men, landing a few paces ahead before hopping and flying into a grassy bush, much to the delight of a bird awaiting its next meal. Doro chuckled at the brief interaction and then pointed ahead. It seemed there was a group in front of them on the road. They didn't appear to be robbers or thieves, but the possibility of the unknown added a tinge of anticipation to the trip.

"Whatever the reason may be," Amias started, "if Elijah has been swept up into a better place, he deserved it. If he's in Naaran, Bethel, Rakkath, or Jerusalem, then there was purpose for it. Regardless, it will be good to learn, find out for ourselves, and then report to everyone else what we learned."

"Agreed," Doro said.

The traveling companions began to approach the group, and they could tell that it was a merchant with his family and a few guards. Someone from the group saw the three men and alerted one of the guards to be on the lookout. Amias could tell when one of the men, who had a large sword on his side, began to move toward the back of the group to see if they were dangerous. As the two prophets and the farmer got closer, the guards relaxed because they could see the trio's robes and assumed no danger. Doro must have looked like a protector or someone who was at least safe due to his choice of friends.

There were three merchant carts with a team of horses pulling each group. Two of them had been carrying wheat, grain, or rye. The third cart must have had family who helped with the business. There were three teens, two of them being the merchant's sons and the other his daughter. A woman dressed plainly sat and talked with her children while a driver controlled the cart and horses. A few men were also on horseback, and the merchant wore blue and maroon robes. Everyone else clearly looked like they were traveling, but he wanted to ensure that he would look impeccable, although that could draw unwanted attention. A few guards walked behind the caravan, but the man in the finely pressed robes guided his horse toward the back as Amias, Afra, and Doro got closer.

"Hello there, strangers; I'm Chagim, a merchant of Rye and metal products," the merchant announced.

Amias could see some of the bundles of rye in one of the carts and assumed the covered one had a similar plant for feed or food. He didn't think it had metal pieces or scrap.

"I'm Amias, prophet for the living God, and this is my companions Afra and Doro," Amias said. "Afra is like me, while Doro is a merchant like yourself."

Chagim's widened eyes told Amias that he assumed Doro did not have that position until it was mentioned. "Where are your goods?" Chagim asked.

"We are on a different mission," Amias started. "One that didn't require our friend's wares or goods to be sold."

Chagim nodded and smiled. "What is your destination?"

"Naaran," Doro said. His voice was commanding and boomed. He wasn't trying to be hostile or mean, but how he drove the words with such emphasis often surprised people. Amias could tell by a second shocked expression that this did indeed happen to Chagim.

"Not for anything hostile or bad, but we're looking for," Amias didn't want to go into detail because they were traveling with a stranger, so he searched the words for the proper term. "Friend."

"In such a small town, I understand," Chagim said.

"Do you sell a lot here?" Doro asked.

"Yes," Chagim said. There was a rush of color that ran across Chagim's face. He apparently loved to talk about selling and making money. Amias assumed this was the case, but then the nicely dressed man made it all the apparent when he went into detail about the road through Naaran, which was perfect for trade routes to Ai, Bethel, and Gilgal. It was near the Jordan River, and, of course, right through the city ran the road they were on. Mostly, it was safe, but there had been reports of thieves. He had never been attacked, but it was worth the money to have the armed guards ensure their goods got to the required destination.

"Your family," Afra nodded toward the woman with the three kids. "They come with you often."

Chagim smiled broadly and said, "No, but when we reach Ai, my daughter is betrothed to a merchant who sells precious jewels and fine robes."

"That's a blessing," Amias said, unsure what to say next.

"Indeed," Chagim said.

In the distance, a man and a few workers were on a large field. Chagim waved in their direction, and someone waved back. The workers were far from the road, but Amias, Afra, and Doro did the same, not knowing whom they were greeting from such a distance. He had hoped it wasn't trouble, but with Chagim's joyful nature, he assumed the people were friendly.

"That's Uwthay's land," Chagim said. "Big-time wheat producer in this area. His children are all over Israel, nice people."

"Good to know," Amias said.

CHAPTER 6

"Where should we begin," Doro asked.

"There," Amias responded, pointing to an inn near the city's center. The inns in Jericho were built for large amounts of people and visitors. In addition to the inn, plenty of homes housed friends, guests, and family traveling in the city. Naaran's inn didn't have a name that Amias could see, except for the words "Inn," "Food," and "Lodging," painted on wooden boards sitting to the side of the place. He wasn't sure if the last two were needed since the word "Inn" would have let guests know what was available inside. Nevertheless, parts of the place appeared that the owners were improving its look and quality. The back end of the building was getting either remodeled or extended. Amias had never been to the city, so he wasn't sure. However, parts of it were being repainted with red and green throughout. The Inn might have been experiencing more customers coming through, especially if Chagim was correct about this little town being on the path to the larger surrounding cities.

Amias knew it was essential to ascertain if the residents or visitors saw Elijah or a memorable event that would have led to him being transported overhead. Amias knew of the chariots but wasn't sure if Elisha meant they stayed in the sky or began to run on the ground. It seemed like an odd description, but Amias didn't want to doubt the veracity of Elisha's words.

LAVAUGHN

The thought of meeting at Elijah's home quickly left his mind once he knew getting a bed and food to eat was necessary. A place like the inn would serve both purposes: gathering helpful information and getting refreshed. The journey wasn't that far, but it still took a lot out of them. Amias and Afra had to admit they were not young men. Amias had just traveled into Jericho a few days before to compound this journey. He had no plans of immediately leaving or going on a long expedition so soon.

The inside of the inn was cleaner than Amias expected. It was decorated with wood carvings, gold and red-colored drapes, tables, and random pieces of artwork. Little items were on the walls and by the cushions that shared the same colors presented throughout the place. It gave the inn a comfortable and inviting feel.

The place to reserve lodging was to the left of the door, while the main eating hall was to the right. Stairs near the entrance headed upstairs to the beds and rooms for rest. Amias took the lead and requested a room for at least three nights. Upon entering the village, they agreed it shouldn't take longer than that to learn if Elijah was in town, came through the city, or wasn't there. After securing their belongings in their room, the three men made their way to the dining area.

As they settled at their table, the tantalizing aromas of stew and cooked meat filled the air. Amias was surprised he hadn't noticed the smell upon entering, but now it was all he could think about. His hunger was immediate and pressing, and he knew he had to satisfy it.

A young woman came to the table soon after the men sat down. She had a pleasant smile whose joy reached her small cinnamon-colored eyes. A red and gold sash around her waist notified the men that she worked for the inn. Amias saw it on her first, then noticed several workers had it on. He couldn't remember if anyone at the inns in Jericho, Hazor, or Rakkath had anything like that. He could only assume that multiple people must have tried to steal objects or food while dressing as servants and workers. Then again, it made it easy for guests to know who was trusted to bring food and drink to their table.

"Hello, I'm Chasida, what would you like to eat?"

"What is that fine aroma that I'm smelling?" Amias asked.

"You too," Doro added. "I've inhaled that scent ever since we walked in."

Chasida smiled and said, "That would be goat and spices stew."

"Three of them, please," Amias said.

"What brings you to town," Chasida asked.

"We're looking for Elijah," Doro answered. He wasn't loud, but his voice carried, and a few people around paused their conversation while eating. A man with thick religious tattoos covering one arm got up from his friends and left the inn. He seemed to excuse himself from his tablemates when he overheard Doro.

Amias thought about Feidi and his warning. What if some Baal worshippers were unhappy with their family members being killed years ago? People could hold on to grudges, especially if that person had someone whose last breath was taken on the banks of the river. Amias thought it would be safer to play it safe in case someone wanted revenge or used them to find Elijah themselves.

"We're just looking for a friend and traveling through the countryside," Amias said. He glanced at Doro and Afra and shook his head. Amias gave them a stern look with tight lips and narrowed eyes. He was hoping to relay a message. Don't mention his name.

"I see," Chasida responded. Her expression dipped from joy to seriousness and then back to pleasantness. She looked around at the table with the missing man and moved a little closer. "There are a few Baal adherents," Chasida whispered. "Beware of Nurim and Nergal."

"Thank you," Afra whispered back.

"I'll get that right for you," Chasida said loudly and returned to the food prep area.

"Sorry," Doro apologized. "I didn't take heed to the warning of my brother."

"Her face said it all," Amias said. He nodded toward the table with only three people when there used to be four. "A man heard you and immediately left to get someone." Chasida's warning was a caution and a signal of potential danger. She had noticed the man's reaction and knew it could lead to trouble.

Afra nodded and whispered, "Is that what changed your tone?"

"Yes," Amias answered. "Chasida picked up on his actions, and that's why she gave us the warning."

"Do you think we can trust her?" Afra asked.

Amias thought about his response carefully. Anyone could be a friend or possible obstacle in their quest. Still, for Chasida to whisper the warning meant she could be helpful in their search.

"Yes," Amias answered.

The goat stew was brought, and the taste was even better than the aroma. Each bite was scrumptious and played with the taste pallet. There was minimal talk about the trip as the men dined sufficiently on the meal and washed it with the beverage provided. They were so engrossed in the food and allowing it to soothe their bodies that they didn't see a visitor come to their table.

"You're not from here," a woman's voice said to the side of their table. All three men looked toward the voice and saw a woman clothed in silks the color of olive tree bark, shades of yellows, and a few silver chains dangling from her neck. Her hands were arrayed with various gems, while piercings lined her ears, nose, lips, and probably several other areas Amias could not see. The air around them seemed to thicken with the weight of her presence, adding to the intrigue of the situation.

"Just visiting, enjoying your city," Amias answered.

"Hmm," the woman said. "I hear you're looking for someone."

Amias' mind searched for who she was. The man who left and returned must have informed either someone else or this person in front of them. Chasida had warned them of two people. She could have been more generalized in her warning.

However, Chasida specifically mentioned two people, which meant they were more dangerous than anyone else in the village.

"And you are?" Amias asked.

The woman bowed and pressed her hand against her chest. "Forgive me, kind strangers, I am Nurim." That was it, Amias thought. Nurim. Her name was definitely one of the ones Chasida mentioned. In reality, there was no reason to trust the servant over this silk-dressed stranger, but Amias knew when to lean on the feeling of when God sends a warning.

"It's a pleasure, Nurim. We're looking for a friend," Amias said.

Nurim smiled. She looked from Amias to Afra, then at Doro, and back to Amias. "A friend," she started. "Name?"

Doro was about to respond and then closed his mouth. He had already made that mistake once, which proved to be helpful with Chasida. However, after their discussion, Amias could see that Doro knew it wouldn't be a good idea to do it again.

"Older man. Might have stuck to the outer areas but would have the look of a…."

"Prophet," Nurim interrupted Amias. The prophet from Rakkath was surprised, and the three men exchanged wary glances. They had not mentioned the prophet to anyone, yet this stranger seemed to know. Their suspicion grew, but they maintained their composure.

"Yes, that's correct," Afra said.

"Have you seen him?" Amias asked, getting over his surprise.

"No," Nurim responded. "But, looking at your robes, you appear to be prophets or religious men yourselves." The three men paused and smiled.

"Does your husband know you are out, speaking with strange men?" Afra asked. "Or does Naaran have a different set of traditions?" To all in Israel and the region, women were rarely allowed to speak so openly to men unless given permission or the men themselves started the conversation. There were exceptions, for example, a servant in an inn, those helping the man for some reason, and, of course, if they were related or a close friend of the family.

"If I had answered in the affirmative that I knew of your," Nurim paused and licked her lips, "friend, would you have asked me such a question."

Afra was about to speak, but Amias intervened. "Thank you for your assistance. We would appreciate the opportunity to enjoy our meal undisturbed. If our friend is absent, we trust he has found safe refuge elsewhere," Amias declared.

Nurim smiled again, even more slyly than before. "Perhaps he has abandoned your God, follower of Yahweh."

"Do not blaspheme His name," Doro said, no longer able to hold back. "There is only one true God."

"Baal," Nurim proposed. She laughed after seeing the men's faces, bringing some attention to the people in the inn.

"Certainly not," Amias answered.

"You believe your God is the one and only, but you should talk with my cousin, Nergal. He is a high priest of Baal in this area." Nurim paused, stared at the table, and then the rings on her left hand. "Luckily for him, he was not a part of the massacre in the Kishon Valley. I spit on the name of the prophet who commenced such slaughter. I lost my husband in that duel."

For Nurim, it was personal, and Amias was relieved that they had not mentioned Elijah's name. Of course, if a person lost a spouse in that manner, they would still be upset and desire revenge. Nurim would do everything she could to go after Elijah, which was probably true for Nergal. Amias was happy that Chasida had warned them of the man as well. He didn't know what Nergal looked like, but at least it was good to see Nurim. Seeing her face taught them who to stay away from and avoid while they looked for Elijah.

"Interesting," Amias said. Nurim looked at them, waiting for a response. Even Doro did not say anything to the spit on the prophet's name comment. Amias could see the recognition of who she was referring to and picked up on the animosity in her voice. The prophet knew the large man was not scared of one singular believer but had no idea in deciphering who else might hold a grudge in the inn.

"What was your friend's name?" Nurim queried. "I can inquire around. It would be no trouble."

"Don't worry, we'll find him if he is here," Amias answered.

"If he wasn't?" Nurim asked. She gently licked her lips and played with a large ring on her hand.

"Then we'll be on our way," Amias responded.

Nurim smiled and said, "You know who to come to for help, and if you would like, there is an amazing grove to Baal. I am a priestess, a position I believe your own God does not grant to women." Nurim smiled once more and left the table.

CHAPTER 7

"The corn isn't going to farm itself. What do you want?" Baruwk said to Amias. This was the eighth group of homes that Amias had interrupted during their work. He did not mean to disrespect Baruwk, who Amias learned of his name through the servant who answered the door. The young man he saw first was timid about getting Baruwk; after meeting the farmer, Amias understood. Baruwk was an older man but carried himself with strength, youthfulness, and vigor. The apparent head of the household was the same height as Amias, but his broad shoulders gave the appearance that decades of grueling farm work made his upper body big and powerful.

Baruwk's greeting matched that of a few of the settlements Amias met. Some were friendly, others neutral, and two of them a bit hostile. The man with the thin beard and greying eyes was on the latter.

"Excuse the interruption; I didn't mean to bother," Amias responded.

Baruwk grumbled something inaudible to Amias and then looked at him in the face. "Go on with it."

"My friends and I are visiting from Jericho looking for a friend," Amias started. He kept the rest short, talking about seeing another prophet like himself who might have come through to Naaran or someplace close. Amias gave the best description he could of Elijah, but every time he did so at the different domiciles, he realized he didn't have the most accurate description. Still, any information the people could muster would be helpful.

Between Amias, Afra, and Doro, he was lucky to have chosen the side of the village he visited. After Nurim came by their table, the trio of men decided it would be in their best interest to learn of Elijah's presence and leave as quickly as possible. Amias figured to go from place to place as a group. Keep themselves safe. However, Afra argued that it would take too long and draw unwanted attention. Doro agreed with Afra, so they split up and went to different sections of the town.

Amias went to the town area, where many of the homes were connected by a large courtyard. Each house had its own family or two living in it, but nearly three to four others were around a courtyard. Behind them was a large field with grain, vegetables, or trees. One house had a variety of animals. Amias realized that with these homes made the way that they were, the city could be self-sufficient if everyone in the town traded with each other.

"Can't say that I've seen anyone that fits that description," Baruwk said.

Amias bowed his head and nodded. "Thank you."

"You a prophet?" Baruwk asked.

Amias was hesitant and unsure of what the man was inquiring about. There was one group of homes that definitely believed in Baal. He could see into the front of the house and saw what appeared to be little idols to the false god. They invited him to enter further, but he kept his questions vague and thanked them for their genuine hospitality. "Yahweh, yes, the one true God," Amias responded.

"About time some of you came through," Baruwk said. "There's an uptick in the others," he whispered.

Amias nodded and smiled. This guy was someone to be trusted—or at least someone he could feel safe with. There was comfort in knowing someone who shared his mindset. Amias found it funny that in his own country, many chose to go against what their people had worshipped for generations.

"I met one of their priestesses," Amias whispered.

"Nurim," Baruwk said and spit on the ground to the side. That was strange, but clearly, the man had no love for the woman. "Her silken dressy ways always put a weld in my throat." The man finished his statement and spit once again. "Over there," Baruwk nodded towards Amias' back right. It was around a large field behind some home. "They do some sacrificing and worshipping. I think. Or they could be relaying stories of wheat sifting."

"Who knows," Amias said and shrugged his shoulders.

"Indeed," Baruwk said and sighed. "I have to go and take care of my corn, but God bless you in finding your friend."

"May Yahweh shine his light forever upon your family," Amias said.

Amias left the farmer's home with a good feeling after starting that part of his trip with a bit of hostility. He knew Afra was on the other side of

THE WIDOW'S OIL

town and Doro stayed near the inn. It was time for them to meet up and give an account for their day. For Amias no one had seen Elijah or anyone resembling the prophet. He was curious to see what his friends had learned.

An old song that his mother sang began to settle in his mind. It was a psalm of David on restoration and healing. He was thrilled to have the comfort and memory of his mother. Her love of God and his father's persistent teaching led the prophet to take the life of being a representative of Yahweh. He had seen the country's decline and wanted to be a part of building it back to what it was meant to be. The journey for Elijah brought joy and renewed purpose in his life. Regardless of the outcome, he would continue to do what he must for the Lord until his last breath.

"You still searching for a friend," Amias heard a voice that startled him out of the songs from his mother. He looked around to his left and saw a tall man dressed in silky robes. The colors were obsidian, fire, and blood.

"Friend?" Amias asked in a tone that he knew was a lie. Of course, he was looking for a friend. But when Amias stared into the deep-set bronze-colored eyes of a man whose piercing glance buried itself in his mind, Amias knew what he had to do. The silk-dressed man was tall, wide, and packed with a well-hardened body. It seemed like everyone in this city must work hard since most of the population he met were solid and muscular. The man wore jewels piercing his ears, nose, cheeks, and hands. Dressed and adorned in the manner that he was, Amias assumed it had to be one person.

"I'm Nergal, high priest of Baal in Naaran."

Amias nodded and continued walking toward the inn with Nergal, the high priest of Baal, following to the left. "I'm Amias, a humble servant for Yahweh, the one true God of Israel."

Nergal chuckled and shook his head. Amias didn't join in the laughter but smiled. He looked just beyond Nergal and noticed a man dressed in an array of oranges. It wouldn't be so noticeable, but most people in Naaran were not dressed in bright colors. Nearly all residents wore shades of brown, grey, worn-out white, and green.

"Am I right to assume you're still looking for someone," Nergal said again.

"Information travels," Amias said. "We're from Jericho and thought to see some of the other towns in the area."

"You met Nurim?"

"Yes," Amias said. He could see the inn many paces away, but it was at least getting closer with each step. Why did he have to go so far? He knew splitting up was a bad idea, but nothing had gone awry until Nergal arrived. He realized that God was with him, and if he could get to the inn, at least Afra and Doro would be there to help with any trouble. "She has the same love of silks as you do."

Nergal laughed and patted Amias on the back. The sudden gesture startled Amias, who, upon realizing that he was not stabbed or attacked, laughed as well. "I didn't know the prophets of Yahweh could make people laugh."

"We're well-rounded and use humor when possible," Amias responded. In the distance was the orange-dressed guy who was clearly with Nergal and another man who wasn't too far behind. However, as he got closer to the Inn, Afra must have gotten there before him and saw himself with Nergal. Walking from the inn and in his direction were his best friend and Doro, who looked like he was focused on bad intentions.

At that moment, Nergal and himself were talking. Amias knew several people loved Baal, but plenty more served God. He didn't want to start a riot in the middle of Naaran due to a misunderstanding between himself and Nergal. Amias stopped and faced the man dressed in various silks, aware of his potential danger.

"Are you offering help or curious about me visiting your town?" Amias asked, his tone betraying his curiosity about Nergal's true intentions.

Nergal's face immediately showed his surprise at Amias' sudden stop. He almost reached for the weapon to his side and relaxed his arms. "Someone believed they overheard a particular person mentioned within your group."

"Who would that be?" Amias asked, already knowing the answer.

Nergal smiled and looked at Doro and Afra, who were heading their way. He shook his head and waved off his friend in the orange and the man nearby. He leaned closer to Amias and whispered, "Some people drudge up painful memories due to some unfortunate actions that took place years ago."

"Your point?"

"It would be a good idea," Nergal whispered and took a deep breath. "Not to mention the man who did such a wretched act in the name of worship."

Amias smiled and leaned in closer. "Maybe some should worship a stronger God," Amias whispered.

The flush of red rushed through Nergal's face and arms. He took another deep breath, saw Doro a few paces away, and turned to his friend. "Be weary, friend," Nergal shouted from over his shoulder. He continued walking to the man in orange and then off to the homes loyal to Baal.

"Nergal, I presume?" Afra asked.

"Yeah," Amias answered.

"Trouble?" Doro asked.

"Yeah," Amias said. "But let's share notes. We'll worry about him and his followers later."

CHAPTER 8

"Are you looking for a friend?" Amias heard a voice to his left say. Amias told his friends about the Baal residents, Baruwk, and, of course, Nergal when the stranger came to them at the city's well. She wore a solid-colored dress with a covering over her head. There were no jewels or excessive makeup on her face. By her appearance, Amias thought it was safe to assume she was a believer of Yahweh or at least didn't follow Baal. The woman stood beside them, looking at the three men and glancing at the well.

Amias, Afra, and Doro were startled. They cut the journey to the inn short and visited the well. It was midday, and most people had already visited the gathering spot earlier. It was possible more would come as the sun continued its descent to the horizon, so the three men believed it would be the perfect place to discuss their day.

As they walked towards the well, Doro periodically looked over their shoulder at Nergal and the man dressed in Orange. Amias even pointed out a different person for them to be wary of. Those men didn't seem to want trouble and went in the direction Amias had come from when asking residents about Elijah.

Afra went first with his mission, and no one saw Elijah or anyone who fit his description. He ran into a few people who were loyal to Yahweh, while a few loved Baal. One person worshiped some

Egyptian god named Apis, while another believed in the Moabite god Chemosh. Afra and Amias were saddened by the plethora of different deities in their land, but that would have to wait to be considered at a different time.

Doro sat in the inn and helped guests and people visiting the establishment. He didn't get much information from people save for Chasida, the servant. She was friendly and would secretly give him helpful knowledge as it came to her. She had not seen Elijah or anyone meeting his description. However, she warned him to tell his friends about possible dangers in the city. Her message would always be said quickly. She mentioned that there was a helpful person who would be from an unexpected situation.

"Allow me," Amias offered and reached for the pot.

"No," the woman responded. But thank you." She pulled water and filled her pot, which was not large but would support at least a few people in her residence. She paused momentarily and, with downcast eyes, repeated, "Are you?"

"Yes," Amias answered. He wasn't sure if she should ask the woman the question he'd been asking others, but with her appearance and the peace he was feeling, she had to be alright. "Have you seen…"

The woman stopped him and nodded towards a path on the edge of a few homes in the forest. "Not out here. But take the path you see and go until you find three large Pomegranate trees in a clearing. There, I will meet you after I return this water home."

Before Amias could respond, she left and headed in the opposite direction of the path she had sent them on. Her mysterious departure left the companions curious and a sense of suspense in the air. Amias looked at his friends, who were as intrigued as he was. With furrowed brows and squinted eyes, Amias shrugged and asked, "You think it's a trap?"

"She feels different," Doro responded.

Afra nodded and spoke. "True. I think she's sincere. Probably have a husband, so she can't be seen talking with strange men."

"Think she has seen Eli...him. Seen him?" Doro asked.

"Only one way to find out," Amias said.

They drank more water and went to the spot in the clearing. The directions the woman gave for the clearing were easy to find, much to Amias's liking. Walking around all day began to take a toll on his legs, and for the first time, he felt his age.

The Pomegranate trees were quite large, and the path was clear. Amias didn't know if it would be a worship center or grove but found the spot peaceful. Still, he wanted Doro to be ready with his weapon in case of an ambush or other problems.

"Glad you made it," the woman said, causing the three men to spin away from the path. She had come from the forest through a partial clearing in the trees. The woman was silent, as they didn't hear her enter the clearing from an alternate direction she gave.

"That's some skill," Afra said, his tone carrying a hint of admiration for the woman's unique abilities.

"I cannot be seen with three strangers; my husband might not approve," she responded, her caution adding to the intrigue of the situation.

Doro elbowed Afra and nodded. "You were right," Doro whispered. Although he tried to be quiet, everyone in the area heard him.

"We are looking for a friend," Amias said. "Have you seen a stranger, an older gentleman, carry himself in a reserved way?"

The woman smiled and spoke. "As though God is with him?"

"Yes," Afra responded.

"I have heard of such a man," the woman said. "Where are my manners? I am Yaffa, daughter of Morichi, from the tribe of Naphtali." This brought a smile to Amias, finding someone from his tribe. It wasn't unusual to see people from any of the twelve groups in Israel, but it always brought joy to Amias when he learned of someone from his homeland in another area.

"That's the woman," Doro exclaimed.

Doro's sudden excitement startled Yaffa and Amias. After his initial response, Amias assured Yaffa everything was okay. Sometimes, Doro's excitement was boisterous, shown in the tone of his words. "What are you talking about, Doro?" Amias asked.

"Chasida, from the inn, said that a woman named Yaffa could be helpful," Doro responded.

"She's a sweet girl," Yaffa said.

Amias was pleased that a trustworthy person talked about Yaffa. Chasida had warned them about Nurim and Nergal. It was good for them to be on the lookout for any possible danger. As before,

Amias believed God could protect them, but he didn't want to put himself in an unfavorable situation to test God's limits. Amias introduced himself, while Afra and Doro followed as well.

"Are you looking," Yaffa paused and looked around the forest for onlookers, "for the great prophet Elijah?"

Amias' heart paused momentarily, causing a momentary surge in his chest and his breath to catch. Could this be the moment he was looking for? Elijah was taken from Jericho and sent north to Naaran. Or was it possible that he came through here on that blazing chariot for the people to see?

"He came through here?" Amias asked.

"No," Yaffa responded. "But there has been talk of him leaving or taken away."

"Talk?" Afra asked.

"Yes," Yaffa answered. "You are not the only ones looking for him. Many people came in last night talking of others, in their villages and homes of multiple men, all looking for Elijah."

"The other prophets," Afra whispered. His tone was quieter, and only Amias could hear him.

Amias nodded. Others must have left as soon as they talked with Elisha. They probably didn't think of Naaran as being all that important but asked around to see if anyone knew of Elisha. Most people probably used the city as a layover to larger towns in the region. Amias figured that would happen and wanted to visit Naaran on purpose. The smaller cities, irrelevant people, or tiny things are often overlooked, but they can provide the most substantial information.

"Is he missing?" Yaffa asked.

Amias and his companions paused. They wanted to make sure to respond accordingly. Although they believed Yaffa could be trusted, they did not want to put themselves in unnecessary danger.

"Possibly," Amias answered. Yaffa's eyebrow raised, and she moved closer to learn more. "According to his apprentice, God took him."

"In a spectacular way," Doro added.

Yaffa looked towards Doro and then back to Amias. She smirked some and shook her head. "Did it have to do with a flaming chariot?"

"A lot has been spoken," Afra said.

Yaffa nodded and chuckled. "Yes, so it's true then."

Amias realized how unbelievable the story sounded. His connection to Elijah and Elisha taught him the impossible can happen. Then again, the story of Elijah winning a significant battle against the prophets of Baal was not taken lightly, and the absence of rain for years also told of a force much greater than the average person would realize.

"According to Elisha, yes," Amias said. "I trust him, so if that's what he said, then I believe it."

"God is great," Yaffa said. "I am sorry that Elijah is gone unless temporary, but I have not seen him here, nor has anyone who came into Naaran."

"I believe that's all we need to know," Afra said.

"You have been helpful, Yaffa; may God bless you," Amias said.

"Before you go," Doro started, "Chasida said. I would be surprised if you were the person that would help. Why is that?"

Yaffa sighed and looked around the clearing. She peered down the path they came on and then at her own. "Beware of my husband, Nergal, and his cousin Nurim," Yaffa warned.

"Husband?" Amias asked.

"Arranged," Yaffa responded. "He gave enough that my father couldn't resist."

CHAPTER 9

"Now what?" Doro asked.

Yaffa left the way she came while the three men took the trail back to town. They offered to protect her, but she thought it would be more dangerous if seen with three men who were not family members. They reluctantly agreed and made sure Yaffa was at least safe until she left their field of view.

Amias was thinking about the difference in the country without Elijah. The Lord might have transported the prophet to another town. There was a slight chance that God moved Elijah to Naaran, but more likely, it would be elsewhere. Still, talking with Yaffa, Chasida, and many others made him realize that Elisha wasn't wrong. The prophets and strong men from Jericho hoped to find someone not meant to be discovered. Elijah had served his purpose and was no longer needed. It was up to people like himself, Afra, Elisha, and many others to pick up the work and continue doing what God needed.

"What do we do now? Should we stay the evening or leave?" Doro asked.

Sensible, Amias thought. Doro was great at getting to the point and living a practical life. Then again, if you are a farmer, you don't have time to think of what-ifs or daydream. There's a field that needs plowing or animals that need feeding. Do the work and reap the benefits.

"Yaffa's warning got me on edge; we should go," Amias answered.

"Tomorrow morning. Right as the Sun breaks the horizon," Afra responded.

"That is poetic, Afra, but clearly, we need to go now. We learned what we wanted to know. Mission completed, let us go to Jericho and relay what we have found," Amias countered.

"You think we can get back before nightfall?" Afra asked.

"Yes," Amias said.

An argument ensued between Amias and Afra. They both believed they were right and wanted to convince the other to go with their decision. Afra said that the day was getting late, they would be tired, and it was unsafe to travel at night with bandits and other troublemakers roaming the roads. However, Amias wanted to take Yaffa's warning seriously. It was clear that multiple people had heard the story of Elijah and Baal worshippers, such as Nurim and Nergal, who would love to enact revenge on some loyal prophets. Amias reminded Afra that Nergal was acting threateningly, and Nurim spat on the ground to curse Elijah's name. Before Afra could mount a rebuttal to Amias' argument, Doro interrupted.

"We have company," Doro said.

Amias was startled by Doro's sudden statement. He assumed that the largest member of their group would go with whichever decision was made between the two prophets. Amias turned his head in the direction of Doro's stare. The large farmer slowly reached for a blunt, homemade weapon. A large piece of wood bulged at the end with a few nodules surrounding it. Doro's movement caused Afra and Amias to pull their bladed weapons from their side. Amias' weapon wasn't as large as Afra's, but it was sharp enough to cut and stab.

Two men stood on the path, a formidable barrier to the prophet's return to Naaran. Amias scanned the area for any other potential threats, but the strangers seemed to be alone. Yaffa's unexpected appearance through the concealed paths added another layer of tension. Amias recognized the man in orange while his companion was shorter and closer. Neither was as imposing as Doro, which did little to ease the prophet's apprehension. He whispered a brief prayer, but his words were cut short by the men's conversation.

"You could put away your weapon," the smaller man ordered. "No need for violence. Follow and tell us about your friend."

"We will gather our stuff and be on our way home," Amias answered.

"No need; we already gather them from the inn," the man said again. "Where's my manners? I am Gakten, and this," the shorter man pointed to his friend, "is Orange. His mother likes the color."

"You stole our belongings?" Afra's question hung in the air, unanswered. No one moved to lower their weapons—not the prophets, the farmer, or the two men blocking their path. Amias tightened his knife grip, silently praying it wouldn't have to be used. The tension in the air was palpable, both groups projecting calm and friendliness while preparing for a potential battle.

Amias' mind drifted to his younger days when he traveled with soldiers. He remembered a time when a few Israelite soldiers clashed with the Philistines. His friend, Phashar, who had since moved to Rakkath, was a formidable swordsman. Amias, on the other hand, was no expert with a blade. But he was determined that nothing would stand in their way of relaying what they had learned in Naaran.

"Our honorable Priest of Baal, Nergal, is holding them safe. We ask that you follow us, and we will take you to him," Gakten answered.

"We've met," Amias called out. Neither group moved towards the other. He could tell nobody wanted to start trouble or get into a fight. This included Orange and Gakten. Although they came across as demanding, it was possible they were not as formidable as he first believed. Then again, he didn't want to assume anything. Amias thought about it from their point of view. They saw one large warrior and two older prophets. Sure, Doro was dangerous, but Amias knew they were assuming Afra and himself were easy targets.

"Lower your weapons," Orange ordered in a gravelly voice.

"Take them," Doro responded.

"Wait," Amias said. Amias didn't know the mindset of the strangers but didn't want to get into a brawl with people he assumed had nothing to lose. He could have been wrong, but he didn't want to get into a fight to find out.

"I agree," Gakten started. "Follow us, and you will return home safely. I promise." Amias saw the sneer on Gakten's face and knew he was lying.

It was possible that nothing would go wrong, but Amias could tell something was amiss. There was a subtle shift in stance. Nothing too large, but his lead leg appeared to be planted in a way that was preparing for an attack.

In the distance, Amias could hear rumblings behind the men and down the same path they used. Multiple people were searching for them, and these two found them walking away from the clearing. No one probably thought Amias, Afra, and Doro would come there. After all, unlike the rest of the town, there were no homes. No one to tell them about Elijah's presence.

Amias didn't trust Gakten's warm voice and kind words. He wasn't sure if Nergal would do them harm or his cousin Nurim. Nevertheless, he wasn't in the mood to find out. He barely shook his head to convey his thoughts to Afra and Doro. Both nodded in agreement. There was no way they were following Gakten and the monochromic man named Orange.

The two men began to move in Amias' direction. He was surprised they didn't call out for help or tell anyone they found the prophets. Arrogance. It's always when you are overconfident about a situation when things go wrong. The two men probably assumed they would win a confrontation and didn't need backup. Amias knew that a fight started by Orange or Gakten meant they had a plan for handling the three men. He didn't know what it was but figured they had some plan of attack to immediately take himself or Amias down and then go after Doro. With that in mind, Amias figured to do the unexpected.

Orange was closer to the group, with Gakten tailing close behind. Doro was not going to let his weapon go, and neither was Afra, who was slowly easing up his stance and appeared to think it was a good idea to go with the two men. Amias thought otherwise.

When Orange was within striking distance, Amias immediately threw his knife, which was embedded in the large man's leg. Orange was surprised and yelped from the sudden pain. He instantly grabbed the projectile, causing him to drop his weapon. The sudden attack startled Gakten enough that Amias could quickly pick up Orange's weapon, which was larger than his own.

Orange pulled Amias' knife from his leg and looked at the prophet. Before he could move, Doro struck the enemy across the head with his club. Doro used this weapon because he didn't want to kill the man. If it came down to permanently ending a fight, Doro had a curved sword strapped to his side.

"You heathens," Gakten yelled. He sliced in Doro's direction and missed. His friend, Orange, was unconscious, so now the fight was three versus one. Afra came from Gakten's blind side and slashed at the smaller man across the arm and chest. Gakten yelped in pain and fell to the ground, dropping his weapon. Before he could make another sound, Doro rendered the man unconscious with a mighty blow across the head.

"Now what?" Afra asked in a loud whisper. He could hear the people not far from their position and assumed they might have heard Orange and Gakten's cries in pain.

"We go home," Amias said.

"How?" Afra asked. "The path is blocked." Afra waved in the direction of the path towards the city. Amias knew it would only be a moment before the two men's delay would cause them to send more people. They had to go, but Afra was not wrong. The path would lead to a severe problem that he did not believe a surprise knife attack would help.

CHAPTER 10

"I can be of assistance," a small voice suddenly emerged from the trees near the three men, catching them off guard. Amias, Afra, and Doro all turned to the voice with their weapons raised. Amias had just pulled his knife out of Orange's leg while they were discussing the way out. Orange momentarily stirred and then went back to being asleep. Amias hoped Doro didn't strike him that he was permanently unconscious, but the sudden movement did relieve any fear.

They could backtrack and leave the way Yaffa did, but there was no guarantee that it was a consistent path or that they could navigate through the trees as quickly as she did. Going past an unconscious Gakten and Orange to the city was a way out, but the three men agreed it wasn't the safest. Amias and Afra were still quietly arguing over what they should do when leaving the city, but getting there was the problem. Then, the quiet voice near them through the trees halted all conversation.

"Is that the servant from the inn?" Doro asked.

"Yes, follow me," Chasida whispered.

The three men paused as they looked around and at each other, unsure of Chasida's true motives. Without another word, Amias moved towards Chasida, who was partway through the trees and pathway. The prophet nodded at the servant while Afra and Doro followed as well.

"I can lead you to the edge of town, near the road that leads back to Jericho," Chasida whispered.

"Why are you helping us?" Amias asked, matching her tone.

Chasida did not answer and held her hand to stop. The thickness of the forest made it hard to maneuver quickly, and all of them got various scratches across their face and body. The trees were thick, but the sun was piercing between the spaces of the leaves and branches. Multiple birds, crickets, and squirrels chimed in their displeasure at the group maneuvering through their home. Amias could see the partial path Chasida was following. He wondered how she knew about going through the trees. Did she learn from Yaffa? Was this a common practice between the residents? It was strange, but he followed in faith, knowing that God offered a way of escape in the impending face of danger. In the distance, more voices were heard of random talk, and Chasida waved them to follow her. No one was going to go elsewhere, but she obliged and continued on her path, and the group's trust in her guidance grew.

"My father was killed due to Queen Jezebel," Chasida said. "I have no love for the prophets of Baal." There was retribution from the Queen, and many of her followers committed violence as well. Amias wasn't sure what Nergal or Nurim would do, but Chasida's statement answered why she was aiding. She didn't care for them, and this was her way of helping believers of Yahweh.

"You know who we're looking for?" Afra asked.

Chasida paused the group once more. There were more distant voices, and then she continued with a smile. "Elijah, of course. Who else could ride a chariot to Heaven."

Prophets and strong men searched parts of the land for Elijah to ascertain where God could have taken him. Searching the various cities and villages, many, like Amias, were determined to see where the Lord could have taken the prophet. Elisha firmly told the men that his master's mission was finished. It was completed, yet they still searched for proof of his departure or that his existence was truly gone from the land. Then Amias comes across a devout of Yahweh by a pomegranate tree and a young maiden who served at an inn and concluded what had been wrestling in Amias' heart the entire time. Elisha was taken to a better place. One of which they all strove to go. Heaven, and with those words from Chasida, Amias smiled.

"Of course," Amias said.

"I saw your tall friend in the inn, asking people about him," Chasida said, referring to Doro.

"Yes, we were on a mission," Doro whispered. He followed the tone of Chasida and Amias. Doro was no idiot. He could hear the people on the path searching for them, and eventually, they would stumble across Gakten and Orange.

"Why do you search for him here," Chasida asked. "Was it to spread God's great blessing for His prophet's work."

Amias did not want to lie but gave a version of the truth that would put his cause in a favorable light. Doro had other intentions.

"We thought he was sent here," Doro whispered. "Did you think of Heaven?" Doro asked either of his companions for the answer. Afra and Amias looked at each other through the branches and leaves and shook their heads.

"It had crossed my mind, of course, but I wanted to be sure," Afra said.

Amias did not respond and shook his head. Afra was lying. He would have said something if his first thought was Heaven. It was a possible and likely conclusion. Still, if that was the first thought, he hardly doubted Afra would have joined them on the journey.

"Sure, okay," Chasida responded. She stopped the group again when she believed she heard something, tilted her head in one direction, and then kept going. "It's not far." The group's anticipation grew as they neared the edge of town, wondering what awaited them there.

Chasida was correct, as her expedition through the forest took them to the path at least 30 minutes from the city entrance. Amias knew they had traveled a tremendous distance but did not know it was this far out. Before the men could thank Chasida, she ran to a rock formation put together by hand. She began to push the rocks on the top and dug toward the bottom of a crudely built hole. Chasida retrieved a sack, hurried over to the men, and gave them a few of their items and a tool to light a torch for fire and direction. The men felt a wave of relief and gratitude towards Chasida for her unexpected help.

"I'm Sorry I could not bring everything," Chasida said. "I can only carry so much."

Amias, Afra, and Doro were surprised that their stuff was salvaged. They looked at one another, then at Chasida. She carried a personal bag and slung it over her shoulder, not making her way back to the city. Then, the three men began to follow her, and Amias looked back at the city and the path Chasida was going. He assumed she would get them out of Naaran and then make her way back, but she was going toward Jericho like themselves. Amias was about to inquire, but Afra spoke first.

"We are most grateful," Afra said. "We were debating on what to do about our things."

"I thought that Nergal had confiscated our items," Amias said.

"Was that a lie?" Doro asked.

"No," Chasida responded. "I'll tell you on the way."

Amias looked at the men and then at Chasida. "On the way, where?"

"Jericho," Chasida said and marched off toward their destination.

CHAPTER 11

"I'd rather get kicked in the face by a horse than marry that man," Chasida replied to Afra's question about her engagement.

After the group gathered their things, they set off on a brisk walk to Jericho. The sun seemed to be cruising faster to get below the horizon compared to its ascent earlier in the day. Despite that, the group of four wanted to put as much space between them and the residents of Naaran. This was especially true once Nergal and his men find Gakten and Orange either unconscious or badly injured. It would probably surprise Nergal that two old prophets and a farmer bested his men. Amias wasn't sure if Nergal would find that impressive or chastised the two for allowing the prophets to escape. Regardless of the Baal's priest's emotions, he knew there would be a strong passion to get them. Amias whispered prayers for the people faithful to Yahweh in case Nergal falsely believed those people were hiding them. None of those people except Nergal's wife and Chasida had anything to do with them leaving. Even more so, only Amias, Afra, and Doro were to blame for defending themselves against the two men on the path. Amias didn't want their actions to get other people interrogated or harmed.

"That bad," Amias said.

"Yeah," Chasida responded.

THE WIDOW'S OIL

The young woman bravely shared her life in Jericho. Chasida detailed how her uncle had arranged a marriage to a man she found neither appealing nor kind. She could have learned to love his appearance, but his behavior and treatment of others were terrifying. She knew her uncle had only accepted the offer because the family had paid twice the bridal price. Despite this, Chasida was determined not to spend the rest of her life in pain, abuse, or worse.

Chasida's determination to help the group was unwavering. She recounted how she had left Jericho and arrived in Naaran, hoping to continue her journey north. She wasn't sure of her destination, only that she had to escape her uncle's control. Despite her fear, she had stayed in Naaran, working at the inn. There were moments when she had wanted to leave, especially with Nergal and Nurim's influence growing in the city. However, she had chosen to stay until the arrival of Amias, Afra, and Doro. From that moment, she knew that when they left, she would return to Jericho and face her family.

"Something happened for you to grab and hide our things," Amias said. It wasn't a question. Amias knew that something caused her to grab their items; otherwise, she would have waited for them to return and left when they did.

"Nurim came in asking if anyone from the staff had seen you," Chasida said.

"Oh," Afra said.

"I was honest, told them I only saw the big guy," Chasida narrated. "But didn't know where you had gone."

Amias nodded and waved. Hevel looked in his direction and then back to Chasida. He paused and stopped the two men. There was something that Hevel had said to his companions that was kept between them. Amias was about to ask Chasida if they were in danger when the head guard returned his attention with a smile.

"Chasida, is that you?" Hevel asked. Now that Amias could see him clearly as they got closer, he was a bald man with a greying beard. His robes were well worn, as he had probably been in the field, ensuring the protection of the workers.

"Yes, Hevel," Chasida said. They greeted one another when they were close, and Amias felt the concentrated stare of his gaze.

"These are..." Chasida started.

"Family," Amias said. Afra looked in Amias' direction and then back at Hevel. Amias knew there was no discussion of their relationship with Chasida. He wanted to avoid unnecessary communication about meeting her for the first time the day prior, how she helped them escape with their belongings, or the reason for their visit to Naaran. To Amias, anyone could be dangerous. He couldn't remember if the merchant mentioned to whom Uwthay was worshipping. Also, Amias was unfamiliar with the relationship of Naaran's citizens. "Escorting her back to Jericho."

"I see," Hevel said. "Returning to your betrothed?"

"We are helping to handle that difficult situation," Afra lied. He smirked at Amias and then returned his gaze to Hevel. Doro looked on the precipice of ruining the masquerade, but Amias' quick elbow silenced him for the moment.

"I see," Hevel said with a bit of doubtfulness.

"We need lodging for the night. Our travels took us away later than we expected," Chasida said.

Hevel rubbed his beard and sighed. He nodded towards the home and walked in that direction. Chasida smiled, and the group of now family followed behind.

Hevel talked with the lead servant who ran the home. They explained the situation to Uwthay, who was pleased to have guests at his home. Upon their entering, Uwthay had his people take them to a room to the side of the central area to wash their feet of that day's dust. Chasida was ushered away to her area while Amias, Afra, and Doro were kept together. They were allowed to relieve themselves from the journey and get clean.

Once they were finished, the group was ushered into the main area with various yellow and green decorations. Most of the walls had drapes that were a combination of both colors. One of the servants helping them mentioned that it stood for life and wealth to Uwthay. Amias was specifically looking for any bullhead gods, statues, or totems in the room. There was none. That omission of the statues eased the tension in Amias' mind and shoulders. The table was carved from an enormous tree as it took up most of the space in the room. To the side was the area where the food was prepared, and Amias could see in the distance where the home extended well towards the back.

A wave of spices and meat thundered into Amias' nose. He wasn't hungry until the scent of food barged into his mind, and his stomach began grumbling. Uwthay and Urit greeted them in the main room, wearing similar colors. The farm had been good to them as the married couple were plump compared to any of their staff or most of the people Amias had seen in Naaran. He didn't think anyone was hungry or starving; many residents were built with muscle. Uwthay and Urit appeared as an older couple enjoying their twilight years while still being head of household at a large farm. Each had jewels on their hands, and Urit had a ring piercing her nose. Both were advanced in age but moved with the grace of a person at least twenty years younger.

"Welcome to my humble abode," Uwthay said. "This is my wife, Urit."

"God be praised," Urit said. That warm greeting brought a smile to Amias' face. He never heard any of Baal's people say the same thing.

Amias and his traveling companions also greeted them with joy and respect. Chasida introduced the three men as family. The longer the hoax continued, the more Amias felt terrible about starting the lie in the first place. Chasida didn't say how they were related. Amias hoped the welcoming couple would assume they were uncles or older cousins.

"Didn't realize you had prophets in your family," Uwthay said. He gestured for them to sit while the servants passed out the food and drink.

"They're from so far away," Chasida replied. "Still, it was good to be amongst family and safety."

The group talked for a while about their trip to Naaran. No one mentioned Elijah or their true mission for finding him. Instead, it was about them going to Jericho to see family and stopping by to retrieve Chasida. To Uwthay, he was thrilled to have guests and told them stories about his adventures and travels throughout the land. Urit often commented or added to Uwthay's tales. There were moments when he would forget a name, a particular place, or even if he had the right outcome with the correct adventure. Urit was always there rubbing his arm, giving a warm smile, and helping with the truth when necessary.

Amias thought it was great to see the couple bounce off each other. He had done a lot in his life but realized at that moment how much he missed having someone there. He was never married but did enjoy being engaged. Amias thought about Afra and his wife and how happy they were. Afra might not have gotten out as much as before, but it never stopped him from feeling at peace and purpose.

Uwthay talked about how he visited Assyria once and even traveled to Phoenicia. It was in Tyre that Urit got the emerald nose ring. It matched the rings on their hands, which Amias realized matched the green and yellow colors decorated throughout their home. Neither Uwthay nor Urit made it to Egypt, but they were happy with where they had been.

Amias had dined sufficiently on the food that was served. They had cooked pheasant with spices bought from Tyre. The vegetables were fresh as they saved some of what they farmed to eat for themselves. Uwthay explained they have a patch of field specifically for the family, workers, and guests to consume. Uwthay and Urit's children moved to Bethel, while the eldest lived in Dan. Despite that, they often came home and enjoyed the abundance of love they could provide.

Before Amias talked about his travels with the Israelite army fighting the Philistines in Gibbethon, a new servant entered the room and relayed a message to Uwthay. Amias wasn't sure what was being said but got concerned when Uwthay stared at Chasida and the supposed three members of her family. Uwthay whispered something to the man, who headed back out of the room.

"My servant told me that an emissary of sorts from Naaran has just arrived," Uwthay said. Pointing in Amias, Afra, and Doro's direction, he said, "They tell me they're looking, for you."

CHAPTER 12

"I can explain," Chasida said. Amias could hear the panic in Chasida's voice. It quivered like the Jordan River and thumped the ears like two Rams fighting for victory. Amias couldn't believe there were emissaries from Naaran. What small town has that? They could have been anyone. He couldn't believe someone from Naaran would come at night. Nergal and Nurim must have been livid to find their people bruised and broken. Amias whispered another prayer for Yahweh believers in that town. He wasn't sure who had the upper hand in the city, but if one side was outraged, they might start a situation, riot, or brawl. Then again, they would and should be safe with God on the people's side. Amias hoped protection would extend to himself and his fellow travelers in Uwthay's home.

"I sent my servant to stall them, but I'm curious to know what's going on," Uwthay said.

"I can really explain," Chasida repeated.

"You must not be family, are you? Did something happen?" Uwthay asked.

"It's not what you think or as bad," Chasida said.

"I don't want any trouble, and if you brought trouble here…"

"Dear," Urit whispered. She gently touched her husband's arm and lightly squeezed it. "Let them talk."

Uwthay patted Urit's hand and smiled. "Forgive my manners."

Chasida began to rush the explanation of the two prophets and a farmer who came to Naaran. She didn't go into detail regarding Elija but mentioned how they were looking for a friend from Jericho.

Amias added to Chasida's story that no one had seen their friend, but Nergal sent people after them. Nergal had his reasons for aggressively searching for them, and Amias didn't know if the residents would harm them for looking for a friend or not agreeing with their beliefs. He thanked Chasida for helping himself and his friends and getting them out of town.

"Thank you, sir, for showing great hospitality when certain residents of Naaran did not," Amias finished.

Uwthay let out a long guttural sigh. The last part got to him. He was a man who believed in excellent hospitality, as it was customary in the region. He went out of his way to help strangers like them and the people from Naaran.

Amias knew that anything could happen. It could get bad quickly if Uwthay handed them over to the emissaries. He didn't think Naaran would enact punishments as Sodom did generations ago. Stories were passed down about how they would commit terrible, inhuman, heathenistic acts of violence on strangers and those who disagreed with their beliefs. However, the people from Naaran might want to discuss what happened with Gakten and Orange. Amias knew there was no way that was true. One man had a knife wound in his leg, while the other quite possibly had a large scar or bruise on his face from being made unconscious. Those two men alone would want recompense.

Uwthay's decision could tip the scales in either direction. He could choose to be fair and send the Naaran emissaries away, ensuring that the two groups never crossed paths. This would be a relief for Amias, but it would also mean sending those people back to a town that was both kind and hateful. The tension in the room was palpable as they waited for Uwthay's next move.

"Hevel," Uwthay called out. Amias looked around, surprised to see the lead guard at the door. The man's sudden appearance, without Amias hearing him enter the room, added a layer of suspense to the unfolding events. He wasn't the servant who greeted the guests from Naaran, but he was there to be by the older couples' side in case trouble arose.

"Take Chasida and her," Uwthay paused momentarily and grinned, "family to the below lodgings in the stables."

"Sir?" Hevel asked.

"I don't want our new guests to know about Chasida and her friends. I'll explain later."

Hevel grinned, nodded, and motioned for Amias and the group to follow him. Each person thanked Uwthay and Urit. Amias recognized that she had inspired Uwthay to have a compassionate heart.

The stables were a large building near the side of the home. Amias didn't realize its size since the front facing the road hid the fact that it continued away from passersby's line of sight. The building could hold several cows, steers, horses, sheep, and goats. The sound of the animals preparing for sleep wasn't as disturbing as the smell. Uwthay kept the place clean, but when dealing with the sheer number of animals in the stables, it would have been impossible to keep the scent as if it were a field of flowers. The animals were grouped by kind, and each had a gate, door, and way to get them in and out quickly.

Below the floor of the stables was a hidden room. Hevel instructed them to be silent as they left the home and entered the stables. Doro marveled at the size of the stable with his approving nods and low hums. In the middle of the stables was a secret passageway below them. What was a door appeared to be a part of the floor until Amias noticed a slight alteration of the floorboards. The opening would have seemed invisible unless you knew what you were looking for.

"If it storms or trouble arrives, we come here," Hevel said. "There are two other rooms like this on the property for safety."

"Uwthay thinks of everything," Afra whispered.

"Indeed," Hevel said. Hevel made sure everyone was safe and comfortable. He informed the group that he would be back when the group from Naaran had left.

The room below the stables was large enough for several people. There were a few old chairs and crude adornments to sit on. A hole was dug to the side where water, food, or other necessities could be kept cool and out of the way. It was dark, but some candles and lanterns could be used for light and heat. Amias would have loved having something to see but had to take what little light was streaming from the stable above. The underground room wasn't below any animals. Uwthay wanted to ensure that no unnecessary animal excrement would fall on the people below. Still, their stench was overwhelming, but Amias preferred that to dealing with the emissaries of Naaran.

Every moment in silence was excruciating. Amias and Afra always talked, and Chasida was an excellent conversationalist. However, the people might want to come to the stables, and hearing people speak below them would have defeated the purpose of hiding in the first place. Everyone wanted to say something. Comment on the situation or make an irrelevant noise. Uwthay didn't have to allow them to do anything in their house, but Amias assumed that Naaran was a major buyer of his goods. The farmer couldn't stop doing business with them, nor did he want to get into a fight. Granted, they did have Hevel, and several other protectors were in Uwthay's employ, but it was better to avoid confrontation. Unless, of course, you have to defend yourself.

Amias began replaying the events from earlier that day in his mind. Did he do the right thing in throwing the knife at Orange's leg? Was there another way God would have gotten them out of the situation? All sorts of passages and stories from the past whirlwind through his head. Amias remembered that Rebecca encouraged her son to steal his brother's birthright. Moses took a life, which sent him into exile from the only home he ever knew. The first King, Saul, decided to save the best for God, only to have it be his ultimate downfall. Did he do as them? Did the two men only want to talk?

Amias sighed long and felt Afra pat his arm. They had been through challenging situations before, but nothing like this. Usually, they were smart about not putting themselves in danger. When they chose Naaran, they searched for the city they believed was close and least threatening. Naaran was close, but there were plenty of threats. Everyone was trying to inform them of Baal believers and how extreme some were. Amias didn't take it seriously but wished he did. Then again, would he not have searched for Elijah? Would he have stopped because some people who disagreed with his belief threatened him? Absolutely not. Amias patted his friend's hand and smiled. Regardless of the outcome, Amias did not regret coming to Naaran or feel it was a mistake to look for Elijah.

There was an extended silence before the voices of Uwthay and Hevel could be heard. Doro almost said something when two other voices streamed from above.

"As you can see, Nergal, no one fitting your description is here," Uwthay said.

"They couldn't have gone far," Nergal said. "The sun is down, and I doubt they would continue their travels in blackness."

"Unless they went towards Bethel or Ai," Nurim said.

"You say they harmed two of your men?" Hevel asked.

"Yes," Nergal responded.

"Two old men and a farmer," Uwthay said. "Amazing."

"Yes," Nergal said once more. There was no pleasure in his tone. It was as cold as the longest day in winter. Amias could hear Baal's priest let out a low sigh. He wasn't sure if he wore the same clothes or changed into something more manageable for a long outing on the road.

"Sorry to have bothered you, Uwthay," Nurim said. "Even the innkeeper doesn't know where his servant girl went. I'm hoping to find her as well. Maybe she knows."

"Maybe," Uwthay responded. "Or coincidence."

"Baal doesn't work in coincidences. We'll find them," Nurim said again, her voice filled with determination. With her declaration, Amias heard footsteps quickly leaving the stables, and the rest of the group followed, their resolve palpable in the air.

The group below the stable collectively sighed, knowing that Uwthay was a man of his word and didn't turn them in. What felt like an eternity was only half an hour later when the group was released from the underground hiding place, a wave of relief washing over Amias and Afra.

Before Uwthay could comment or say anything, Amias hugged the man and thanked him profusely. "May God bless you more than you can imagine," Amias said, his voice filled with gratitude and emotion.

"He already has," Uwthay said. "I'm returning the favor to His people."

CHAPTER 13

"I wish there were more we could do for you," Amias said to Chasida as they prepared to leave her uncle's home in Jericho.

The group was safe the previous night while lodged in Uwthay and Urit's home. Everyone knew that Nergal and Nurim would search for them in other cities. Nurim had mentioned Bethel and Ai, so Amias hoped they would go there. Eventually, the Baal priests would forget about them and move on to more pressing matters. Amias had no idea what could distract them but assumed the cousins would continue to search for Elijah themselves or try to convert others to their god. On the trip to Jericho, Afra mentioned Gakten and Orange seeking revenge. Doro wasn't afraid because he knew those two were low-level scrubs that wouldn't be a problem. Amias wasn't as confident but had faith that God would protect them.

After the night had been broken by the new day sun, the four people made their way to Jericho. Their conversation meandered from Naaran to the events at Uwthay and Urit's home, farming, rumors of wars, and Chasida's personal life. Amias knew that her family was trying to do what was suitable for her and themselves by attaching to a wealthy family. They were looking out for now and the future.

Afra suggested that they could not allow Chasida, who had been instrumental in saving their lives, to be married to an abusive man. Chasida was okay with being at peace with her uncle and mother's decision. She wanted to see her family. Afra didn't want to accept that situation, nor did Amias.

When they got to Chasida's home, they were greeted by her mother, Jaleh, and Uncle Mihram. The house was quaint, with a rounded room that served multiple functions. It was the gathering room, a place to prepare food and sleeping quarters. There were smaller rooms to the side of the home that Amias understood as another place to rest. Most of the furniture was handmade by the family. Chasida's mother, uncle, a few cousins, and a close family friend stayed in the home. They had various jobs in Jericho, from farmer, fisherman, weapons apprentice, and horse caretaker. Some women helped the rich with nursing and raising their children, while others did something with herbs and plants.

There were no signs of Chasida's betrothed, which was understandable. They had no way of knowing she would return on that specific day. Her family was happy to see her but surprised at the prophets she came with. After the pleasantries and excitement, Mihram wanted to talk with Chasida alone and how she would be honor bound to their arrangement. He was furious with her for embarrassing the family. Amias understood his frustration. He wasn't sure if Chasida's actions would spread through other cities, causing them to lose hope of getting a bridal price or the previous family backing out of their commitment. Then, the unexpected happened.

"I have a man who is Chasida's age. He's a hard worker, intelligent, good with his hands, and will treat you and your niece with respect," Doro boomed.

"What?" Amias asked. There was no talk about Doro marrying one of his men to Chasida. Amias knew there were plenty of people on his farm who needed wives. Everyone kept having males, which was suitable for labor, but he also needed women. Chasida would make any man thrilled. She was young, but Amias could see she was attractive, intelligent, a great communicator, and brave. The children she would make with one of Doro's strong workers would be impressive.

"I am more than willing to pay more than what was offered," Doro proclaimed. He looked at Chasida and said, "She has shown herself valiantly in times of stress. We would be honored."

No one at Chasida's home was as large or imposing as Doro, so his words and money ended the negotiations. Plus, she would be close to the family since Doro only lived a partial day's journey outside Jericho's walls. The amount was agreed upon, and Chasida was now engaged to a robust and youthful man on Doro's farm.

"You have done quite a lot," Chasida said, responding to Amias. "I'm looking forward to seeing my husband soon," Chasida said to Doro with a grin.

"You will be well pleased," Doro responded.

****

Amias, Afra, and Doro were among the first people to return from their journey. They had not gone as far as most, so Amias figured that would be the case. He planned on being in Jericho for a while before the council, meeting with Elisha, and exploring Naaran. Amias enjoyed being in the company of his friend and got to know more about the town's residents. Once most people returned, it was apparent that Elisha had spoken the truth. Khahea, Meonothai, and dozens of others returned, saying that no one had seen Elijah in any of the towns they visited. News began to spread of him leaving, but that was probably due to the fifty-plus prophets and strongmen inquiring around the region. After everyone had said their piece, it was clear. God took Elijah away because it was time. He had completed the given mission, and it was time for others to proclaim Yahweh as the one true God in the land.

After the men had given their report, Elisha said, "Did I not say to you, do not go?"

He was right, and everyone knew it. Still, it was good for them to see and learn for themselves. Amias wasn't thrilled that it could have put them in danger, but they did get to help save a young servant from a possible abusive situation. Doro received an excellent bride for one of his workers, and they were able to befriend a wealthy landowner not too far from Jericho.

When returning from meeting with Elisha, Amias sat in Afra's home for a while, staring at his walls. He wasn't focused on the furniture, Bara cooking the next meal, or Afra coming to his side. His mind went to Uwthay and Urit. On the trip back, he thought about their love, her compassionate touch, and how Uwthay was a happier man with her in his life. Amias wasn't sure if Uwthay's existence was better, considering he met him only a few days before, but there was a sense of peace. Amias was at peace with his life until he was around Afra on this trip and meeting Uwthay. He was engaged, but it ended when his betrothed passed away due to a terrible accident at her parent's home. Since then, he has thrown himself into working for the Lord. Amias traveled from city to city, representing God and ensuring Yahweh was known despite the growing worship of false idols.

"Amias," Afra called out.

"Yes," Amias responded. He said it in a tone that was hazy and slow.

"Did you hear me call you?" Afra asked.

"I need a wife," Amias said. Afra was about to respond but stopped with his mouth wide open. He closed it, hesitantly opened it again, and said, "What?"

"God is letting me know. It's time," Amias responded.

"For a wife?"

"Yes," Amias answered.

Afra nodded his head and looked over at a stun Bara. She glanced at the two men and then returned to cooking. "There are some families around with available maidens. I can ask around," Afra started.

"No," Amias said. "I must go home."

"Hazor?" Afra asked.

"No, Rakkath."

THE WIDOW'S OIL

****

Amias didn't leave Jericho immediately, staying with his friend for an extra week. After that short moment, he went and traveled home. He talked with God during the entire trip. He devised a plan for what he would do while in Rakkath and how he could be of use. There was an idea of possibly starting an olive grove and farming. He was going to do what he could to prepare for a family. Amias hoped the residents would also pay for some of his salary through donations and gifts, but it had been a while since living in that city. He knew Phashar, a friend from his youth, and several other families were there. However, he didn't know if he would go to a town devoted to Yahweh or other gods like some of the people in Naaran.

Amias lived a simple life and had plenty of savings. There would be no problem with a bridal price or showing the family that he would care for their daughter. He knew his wife would have to be years younger than himself. Amias felt active but knew his wife would have to be young to have his children. She didn't have to be Chasida's age, but someone in her twenties. Amias knew it would be tough to find such a woman of value. Usually, families try to get their daughters married as soon as possible, much like what happened with Chasida. However, the youngest daughter in a line of sisters often had to wait for their older siblings to get married before the father would arrange her union.

When Amias arrived at Rakkath, he noticed that the town had grown. There were more homes and businesses towards the front of the city. Being near the Sea of Galilee was a significant boost for the economy. He had learned that Upaz, the richest resident in the town, was growing a major trading and merchant business throughout Israel. The Inn was larger than he remembered before, which allowed him to find a perfect place to relax and be able to send for his items in Hazor.

While in Rakkath, Amias learned a home for visiting prophets was available. He planned to stay in the visitor home after a few days in the inn. The mayor mentioned that a new home was for sale near a recently married couple named Tamir and Shireen, which changed his mind. Amias visited the house and knew it needed work but was more than willing to do what he could. The bonus was that Shireen's parents lived in Hazor, and Amias knew them. They were wealthy landowners in the town and were kind to him whenever he would visit or see them around town. Amias was well pleased with the direction of his life. Amias stayed at the inn for the first week and then moved his travel things to the new home. His belongings from Hazor came to the town a few weeks after he had fixed and cleaned the house. Tamir became an excellent neighbor and helped with much of the repairs. Phashar would stop by with his wife, a Nubian out of Egypt. She informed him that she knew various medicines and herbs to help if he was ever in need. Through Tamir and Phashar, he learned of the city's multiple residents, which allowed him to be friendly and get to know the people.

Tamir had mentioned one person who sounded like the perfect candidate to build a family.

THE WIDOW'S OIL

He never saw her around the city but did meet with her family, who were thinking of leaving Rakkath. One of the woman's sisters lived in Egypt, while another had passed away.

After a grueling moment of preparing his land for trees, Amias went to the well to get refreshed. The day was temperate. He expected it to be hot and burdensome, but it wasn't to his delight. At the well drawing water was a young woman with a comely face. Amias could tell by how the clothes wrapped around her body with the wind that her hips were perfect. It highlighted her figure that accentuated a small waist and ideal chest. There was a pleasant smile in the corner of her lips turned up while a sparkle in her eyes drew him in. She easily pulled the water from the well with a concentrated demeanor. She reminded him of Chasida, but a few years older with a bit of wisdom. Amias couldn't figure it out, but the woman looked like someone who had gone through the fires of life and came out stronger.

"Excuse me, miss," Amias said.

The woman was startled at Amias' sudden presence. She glanced over his face and robes and then back into his eyes. She softened—not much, but a little. Her stance, a bit more open, was inviting instead of one meant to attack.

"Is your husband not around to draw water for you?" Amias asked.

"No," she responded.

"Is he at war or in a faraway land?"

The woman shook her head. "I have no husband, but I help my family by any means."

Amias barely heard the rest of her statement after she admitted to not having a husband. Could he have found the person so fast? Amias was surprised to hear that someone her age was not betrothed, but that did not stop him. He wasn't sure what her character was, but he wanted to know more.

"Do you need help?" the woman said, motioning toward the well. "I'd like to be of service."

Amias grinned and rubbed his brow. That's all he needed to hear. Someone willing to help a stranger was someone worth knowing. "All I need is your name?"

"Mary."

Made in United States
Orlando, FL
03 October 2024

52331964R00071